ASUNDER

A Story

PART ONE: *ENTER THE FIRE*

INFINITY PUBLICATIONS PRESENTS

MS. JEWELS

the ASUNDER *Story*... **PART ONE: ENTER THE FIRE**

the ASUNDER *Story*...PART ONE: ENTER THE FIRE

The Asunder Story © Copyright 2022 by Jewels Clark. No part of this publication may be reproduced, distributed, or transmitted in any form or by any means, including photocopying, recording, or other electronic or mechanical methods, without the prior written permission of the publisher, except in the case of brief quotations embodied in critical reviews and certain other noncommercial uses permitted by copyright law. All rights reserved.

This is a work of fiction. Names, characters, businesses, places, events, locales, and incidents are either the products of the author's imagination or used in a fictitious manner. Any resemblance to actual persons, living or dead, or actual events is purely coincidental. For permission requests, write to the author, addressed: "Attention: Permissions Coordinator," at the address below.

Vanderbilt Media House
Infinity Publications, LLC.
999 Waterside Drive
Suite 110
Norfolk, VA 23510
(804)286-6567

∞ Infinity Publications ∞

www.vanderbiltmediahouse.net
Library of Congress Control Number: 2019277106
ISBN-13 : 978-1-953096-29-6
First Edition : June 2022
10 9 8 7 6 5 4 3 2 1
This book was printed in the United States

LGBTQ READS

the ASUNDER Story...PART ONE: ENTER THE FIRE

Note from Author

This book was conceived in a dark time in my life. Yet a guiding light revealed to me that I had something to express. I would do it in a way that is subtle but enlightening for my people to understand that no matter our plights in life, when the Creator brings a togetherness about our misunderstanding of how we view each other, it is for the common good of our humanity.

We are all one family in this world, we became asunder by neglecting the fact that you should never underestimate the powers of forgiveness. Let us love on each other. We are all the same from my sister to brother.

the ASUNDER *Story*...PART ONE: ENTER THE FIRE

Dedication

To my young ones: David, Gweneth, Joshua J., and the Matriarch of us all-Deborah J. Clark, my mother. Without the Creator and the people thus the purpose of the project wouldn't exist. Most importantly I must say thank you to Ms. Winter Giovanni (my publisher), for giving me the opportunity to change my life in this lifetime.

the ASUNDER *Story*... PART ONE: ENTER THE FIRE

Prologue

"Lockdown time! Lockdown time everybody. Now!" Cried the rinky dink correctional officer.

"Damn Lil bro. I gotta go. I'll call you next week sometime. A'ight?" Semaj said to his little brother Daniel gloomily. Daniel was his oldest brother's biggest supporter and friend in life. And right now, prison stood in between them.

"Okay Semaj. I love you big bro and stay strong," Daniel expressed.

"Ok love you too bro. Peace," he said hanging up the phone. He surveyed his new home and took a deep sigh. This was his place of residence for the next five to ten years. And that solely depended on the parole board and himself.

"Room 206, Mr. Carter. Lockdown time man, come on!" The C/O sounded irritated, yelling directly at him bringing him into 'the now.' He also put him under the spotlight, which he did not care for any of the attention.

He strolled over to his cell taking his precious time. As he approached the cell, the officer appeared irrational and ready for confrontation. And the officer wasn't holding back with the tongue either.

the ASUNDER *Story*... PART ONE: ENTER THE FIRE

"You think you can move any slower there, boy?"

"Man, what the fuck ever!"

"What did you say?"

"You heard me!"

"Nah...I didn't because I don't speak nigger lingo..."

"What?! Man, who the fuck..." The brewing quarrel was interrupted by the individual that occupied the room with Semaj.

"Aye, lemme holla at you young gangsta," he replied.

"Come on inside the cell youngin. Don't feed into that foolishness. It's pointless," the man exclaimed.

The corrections officer stood aside from the door. He looked the C/O over thoroughly before stepping through the threshold into the cell. Once he entered the room, the steel door slams behind him almost simultaneously, barely missing his heel. No sooner than he jerked around, the C/O was gone.

He walked over to his bunk and plopped down hard. Besides the noise generating from the man's headphones, the room fell quiet. He leaned back on his rack, watching the man in the chair. The man seemed too poised. He appeared to be about thirtyish and very soigné, almost to measure to be in prison. The *'Belly of the Beast'* didn't give a shit who it swallowed up, digested, and regurgitated out.

the ASUNDER *Story*...PART ONE: ENTER THE FIRE

The man was reading a business magazine and watching the news.

A fake ass black politician, Semaj thought to himself and grinned from his presumption. The man soon broke his silence as if he could sense Semaj's vibe.

"What's your name young gangsta?" He asked.

Semaj really wasn't in the mood for conversation but figured what the hell.

"Semaj," he uttered. The man was very persistent.

"This your first bid?"

"Yeah..."

"Listen youngin, you're on a spot where these whities will handle you if you let 'em. You dig?"

Semaj wondered where this was going. "I hear you. What's your name old school?" he asked facetiously.

The man smirked before answering. "GS," he responded simple and plain.

"What does the *GS* stand for old gangsta?" He decided right then that he would deal with GS in the same way he was trying to deal with him. Maybe that might slow down his momentum a little bit.

"Godfrey Divine Sevens, Sevens with an '*S*' at the end," Godfrey commented calmly. The tone was set. Or was it?

the ASUNDER *Story*... PART ONE: ENTER THE FIRE

Was there tension in the air? It was hard to tell, they both seemed defiant.

Semaj closed his eyes. His mind began to drift. He was out in the streets pounding the bricks with the vices and thugs that partook into the fabric of the street life.

GS intruded into his thought, almost seeming eager to interrupt his state of mind. "You can't do it like that young gangsta."

Semaj sighed noticeably. This gangsta shit was getting on his last nerve.

"Do it like what kid?" he said feeling compelled to press some of GS's buttons with some of his own antics. Curiosity began to get the best of him.

"You can't do it like that. Being in them streets, while you're in here. That shit'll drive you to the mad house to crash-n-burn. Matter of fact, these are your new streets. Get used to 'em."

Matter of fact what? This shit was getting outta control, he thought. He took in everything he told him, except that last part.

The 'matter of fact' part of his comment seemed as if he meant more harm than help.

Semaj was slightly indignant. "Yo B. You got somethin'

the ASUNDER *Story*...PART ONE: ENTER THE FIRE

you tryna get off your chest?" he said as he was sitting up on his bunk preparing for a confrontation with GS.

GS seemed too calm, but stated his claim sternly, never putting down his magazine.
"Listen youngin," his agitation soon became apparent.

"My name ain't Kid, B, or any of that other fly shit you're spitting out of your mouth. It's Godfrey Divine Sevens and they call me GS around here. You dig...for the second time?"

Ahh man. This was all that he needed.

"And my name ain't Young Gangsta. It's Semaj Raymond Carter, but my peoples call me Freedom!" He said as he began to erect his body from the bunk.

G.S. never moved. Maybe out of fear or he just didn't feel threatened. "Okay, okay Freedom. Be easy. I got you." He mildly responded, in some foreigner's accent. Freedom sat back down on his bunk but not before making it known he ain't 'nothin to fuck with. G.S. put down the magazine he was reading, picked up his remote, and turned the television to B.E.T. Then unhooked the headphones to his television so the young man could hear the television as well; however, Freedom didn't care for the gesture.

The mood between them had been set. Freedom laid back on his rack but kept GS in his peripheral. The water had been drawn, but neither of them would drink of it tonight.

G.S. was aware of everything, so it seemed. And when he said his next comment to Freedom, he was almost surprised. It felt like the man didn't miss a beat.

"It ain't me you gotta keep an eye open for Freedom. It's the police and these niggas that act like op's that you gotta watch out for. You feel me?"

Freedom didn't say a word. He didn't have to. He was in prison now. He was fresh, but he'd be damned if he was gonna be somebody's fresh meat. He knew he was gonna survive; however, he had just entered the fire. And the furnace was already hot.

the ASUNDER *Story*...PART ONE: ENTER THE FIRE

PART I

the ASUNDER *Story*... PART ONE: ENTER THE FIRE

Chapter 1

the ASUNDER *Story*... PART ONE: ENTER THE FIRE

The Bait

"Wake up call for chow! Wake up call for chow!" A voice blared from out of the intercom system yelling into every cell inside the building.

G.S. was already up watching CNN News. Freedom got up and released some urine damn near the color of chicken broth. Remnants of 'Mary Jane' was evident in his system. He smoked plenty of weed in jail. Prison was a different beast in and of itself. He might need to clean himself up, considering the confrontation that happened with him and the C.O. last night.

"Water," he said silently to himself.

GS got up and left the room without saying a word to him. He also left his television on. Freedom dared not to touch it. For all he knew, he could have been trying him to see what he would do while no one was watching.

"This motherfucka thinks he's got all the sense," he said to no one in particular.

He put on his sneakers, which were a fresh pair of Nike Air Force Ones. He noticed a black scuff mark on the back of his left shoe. "Da fuck!" he mumbled thinking maybe the door did catch his heel or maybe GS might have marked it. Although he didn't think that the man was petty in that aspect. However, you could not put anything past anybody nowadays...especially a prisoner. He took a rag and dabbed at the mark because he knew wiping the stain could smear it. And he had to preserve these sneakers until he received some money on his books.

His mother mentioned that things were tight in her financial world. He remained patient though. She knew God would always see them through. That was his mother's motto. God did not have to preserve these shoes, either. And in Heaven, bare feet seemed essential walking around on puffy cotton. He chuckled at his thoughts then left the room to head for chow.

While walking to the diner hall, he took in the early morning spring air as if he were inhaling a fresh Newport cigarette. The slight breeze encompassed him like it was welcoming him to the penitentiary life ahead of him.

When he stepped inside the chow hall, he recognized a few faces although none of any importance. As he was getting in the line, a few transgenders were making frivolous gestures while mumbling under their breath about him.

"Umphh, girl. Ain't that nigga fine?" One of them said while licking her lips.

"Yes, girl and he's sharp from the top of his head to the

bottom sole of his shoes gurl."

Freedom didn't pay that shit any mind. As he was getting his food, he heard someone calling his name. He got his tray, grabbed a couple of condiments, turned around and noticed GS flagging him down. He smoothly strolled over to the table where his new celli were located. After sitting down, he was greeted by two other old timers.

"What's up young gangsta?" One of the men asked.

Freedom looked at the man and wondered what was up with these old clowns and this 'gangsta' crap. He also wondered if GS rigged up the conversation. Finally, he responded.

"What's up old school?"
The other guy just nodded his head. Then GS spoke.

"'Yo, Lil Mike and Fuzzy! This is my new celli. His name is Freedom." Freedom was glad that he wasn't on the type of time like he was last night. Both old heads at separate times stuck out their fists to bump fists with him. He took this as their formal greetings, and he returned the gesture, dapping them both up.

As they commenced to eating, a transwoman came over to their table and whispered something into GS's ear. He nodded in agreement at whatever the queen was saying to him.

the ASUNDER *Story*... PART ONE: ENTER THE FIRE

Freedom watched with hawk eyes. He wasn't so much as bothered that the queen came over to the table where he was sitting; more or less, she was one of the transgenders that was talking about him entering the chow hall. He kept eating trying not to be disgusted by the entire ordeal taking place at the table.

After the queen left, Freedom glanced over at GS not necessarily for a response; however, he gave him one anyway.

"That was Mercedeez letting me know that her man, I mean his man will be here shortly to pay off some of the debt he owes."

The table fell silent. Suddenly some bumb looking guy came to the table and squatted beside GS.

"Yo, yo wus happenin captain?"

"Yo, Smurf you got my scratch?" He was clearly aggravated.

"Got damn GS why you..." GS cut him off in mid-sentence. "Muthafucka if you ain't got my scratch or my bud get the fuck away from this table and go get my shit!" GS snarled.

Freedom couldn't help but to snicker at the situation for it reminded him of the movie 'Friday' when Big Worm confronted Smokey about the same shit. Smurf handed him a small pouch. HE passed it off to Fuzzy, who opened it up. He looked, closed the pouch back up, looked at GS and nodded. He nodded back and raised his hand as if he was getting ready to smack the shit out Smurf. Smurf ducked out the way almost stumbling to the floor, but quickly regained his balance, and slid off casually. GS burst into laughter.

"Got damn Smurf which one of ya'll wearin' the panties you or the bitch Mercedeez?"

Smurf didn't respond, but he looked around to see if anyone had noticed the ordeal. He was glad no one was paying attention, so he thought.

"Damn GS you might as well make him yo bitch." Lil Mike jokingly expressed.

When GS looked at him with a sinister look Lil Mike's smirk quickly vanished off his face. From what Freedom had noticed for the last ten minutes was GS had some type of manipulation ingenuity. He still wasn't impressed.

The chow hall begins to clear out. Their table stayed seated. A beguiling white C/O walked over to their table. She was quiet stunning in fact. She had a beautiful voluptuous derriere, a petite set of breasts, an almond angular face, with golden orange curly locks.

"How long you and your entourage gonna be?" She asked him showing off a row of luxurious pearly whites.

the ASUNDER *Story...* PART ONE: ENTER THE FIRE

GS smiled in sync and asked her how long she think they should be. She almost became flirtatious, until the little wild ass pip-squeak C/O from the previous night popped up, seemingly out of thin air. He was blowing his loud little whistle all amplified, and quickly approaching their table.

"Oh lord there he goes...Im'a talk to you, I mean Im'a get with you later GS" she slightly mentioned to him with a subtle eye wink. Freedoms eyes followed her figure all the way out the door, before being interrupted by GS.

"What, Freedom you ain't seen snowflakes fall from heaven like that shit there huh?"

GS obviously didn't miss a beat. Freedom was almost offended. Godfrey paid too much attention to him and that could be a potential problem.

They got up and begin to leave the diner hall. On the way out the door little C/O geek squad ran down on Fuzzy, like he was tryna get the muthafuckers autograph.

"Excuse me Mr. Reynold's sir! Get your ass on that there fence and lemme pat you down!" he exclaimed.

Fuzzy got on the fence and spread eagle. He was so eager to catch him slipping that he never noticed the small pouch in between the crevices of his fingers. After a brief search he told Fuzzy to carry his ass. He turned around looked

the ASUNDER *Story*...PART ONE: ENTER THE FIRE

at the officer with a daring stare as he walked away. It was almost like a challenge that the officer quickly refrained from. Not once did GS stop to see if his partner got snagged up. Freedom took it that he knew Fuzzy was on point and therefor never looked back.

"Freedom come here youngin," GS said to a startled young convict.

"Listen that old school gangster there been getting away wit shit on this spread for years...he got life when he was 21...he fifty-two now, been on this compound for thirteen years. He knows how to move trust and believe."

Again, GS was in his thoughts. Oh, shit this nigga was airtight wit game, and everything else that came within his circumference.

"Yo GS how long you been doing time my G?" Freedom asked him wondering how sophisticated his mind truly was.

"Shit Freedom bout seven-n-half years...been on this joint bout four years...and gotta bout a hundred thousand years left...you smell me...But nah seriously it's gonna take a miracle to open the flood gates for the God."

"Damn what your life been like for you to deserve that type of treatment?"

the ASUNDER *Story*...PART ONE: ENTER THE FIRE

"Freedom, I'ma entrepreneur who's gain in life surpassed my peers and for that my dude I am detrimental to society...I'ma rap to you in a bit bout a nigga situation eventually, when we get in that 6 by 8."

"My father ran an ironclad cartel with some of his Trinidadian peeps and they were vicious as fuck. That's another story though...anyway Romelio Kayne Sevens never did more than 48 hours in a cell. The only reason that happened was he was so inebriated the op's who picked him up that night couldn't let him drive to his home. Once they figured out that it was the infamous Romelio them cocksuckers couldn't wait to put him in a cell. They had this thing for catching my pops. And my guy, they tried everything under the sun to lock him up and throw away the key...moral of the story is after his death I took over the family business...The Almighty Sevens Attire, became my playground. Our blood became like water when my dad passed away...my mother felt like he'd leave all our inheritance to her...and when he didn't, she became the meanest winch you couldn't stand. I know.... that's life though.

I'm the second to the oldest of three. One of my siblings I've never met; more-or-less I seen her in a photo with so much of our resemblance. She's a child Rome had outside of my old

the ASUNDER Story...PART ONE: ENTER THE FIRE

earth. Let me get you to the reason I'm telling you this shit young gangsta. My oldest sister Amera and myself was transporting a little over two kilos in a hidden compartment in our ride on that fucked up day. We were just getting off the New Jersey turnpike and was pulled over. Supposedly our left rear light had a dim glimmer...bullshit I know. What's strange is I don't know if my sister got out the car and told them some foogazy shit 'cus in the end I was the only one tryna get outta the county jail. And you know what my nigga I ain't seen outside since. She claims she never said a word to the D's and boys, but here I sit waiting to step back on dry land. You do the math young gangsta."

As they approached the unit Fuzzy was just strolling up to them and passed the small pouch off to GS Freedom was taken aback from the coolness of Fuzzy's persona. GS even carried his air like a subtle mist of an untamed gangster. It's obvious why he almost finished every sentence with young gangsta. Both were two calm and collected to be in here with him. At least that's what it seemed like to Freedom.

After getting back to their cell GS asked him did, he deal with the essence. Freedom looked at him with this spaced-out look.

"My guy, does you smoke dis gasoline or not. Stop acting

the **ASUNDER** *Story*...**PART ONE: ENTER THE FIRE**

like you a rookie young nigga and hit this." GS commented with a slick look on his face.

"You light it up first then GS." Freedom said sounding a bit skeptical.

"Hoh yeah, okay!" GS exclaimed coolly. He lit up the stick, puff puff and passed. Freedom hit the stick a couple times as well. After passing it back to GS he immediately started sweating profusely. He walked over to the door and peeked out the window. What the fuck was this? What did he have in this shit? GS was watching him keenly. Then he asked him had he ever been to heaven on the spice mobile.

"Man, what the fuck is in this weed old nigga!" Freedom asked him, feeling hazy as hell and a bit mad.

"It's called spice one young nuts and that shit is not a game...you can't be hittin' that shit like it's ordinary smoke."

Freedom walked away from the door and laid on his bunk thinking to himself that this is the first and last time he'd ever smoke anything with this nigga. His head started spinning like the Wheel of Fortune. He tried closing his eyes which was a bad idea.

"Damn GS I should fuck you up for not telling me this was some goddamn spice!" he uttered probably quietly because he didn't even hear himself say what he imagined he just said.

"Shut the fuck up young nigga and relax I ain't make you hit the shit!" GS spat back with a cynical laugh. All he could do was look at the man in frustration. Forced to close his eyes and not think of all the ways in which he wanted to kill GS now, lead to a drift and he dreamt.

'Semaj and his sister hadn't spoken to one another in a few days, but siblings always went through that type of shit. You brush your shoulders off and kept things moving.

This one night his mom had been texting him and trying to get in touch with him for hours. He had been in the studio laying down some ambitious bars. So, when he finally did check his texts and seen his mom had been texting him back-to-back, he immediately knew something wasn't right. When he finally called her, she was frantic and irate. He had to scream on her to chill out so he could better assess what the hell was going on. Her claim was that his sister had got into a serious altercation with her child's father. And that wasn't the woes of it all he put her out, and she had been walking around somewhere in Philly. Ah nah dis nigga didn't. No matter what they had been going through a few days before that she was his sis and he never put his hands on her. He assured his mom that he would check shit out, but he wasn't going to get involved.

He immediately left the studio and headed to Philadelphia. Nothing was on his mind but what he wanted to do to the nigga.

He found Antwan's place immediately, thanks to the journey he made two weeks prior. He had taken them there two weeks ago, after Antwan's car hadn't started. He only had $40 to cover a trip way out to Philly, but because it was his sister, he drove them there. Now he was glad he took them.

He pulled in the back of a Suburban three houses down from where Antwan lived and waited. It wasn't long before Sariah strolled out the door with her luggage and Antwan behind her appearing to be talking big shit to her. A lover's quarrel, one that he really didn't want to get involved with. That's just what couples did at times. Now he wasn't prepared for the next few things that happened. Antwan got in her face and was yelling at her the whole while her head bowed as if he was King Tut or some goddamn body. Okay he could even tolerate that. But when he got really close enough to her face, he spit on her then smacked her down to the ground. Oh God it took everything in him not to hop out his car and blow his face off the map. Sariah seemed to be on the ground holding his leg as he excused himself from her presence. Then Antwan turned around and kicked her off his leg. Now he was irate beyond rationale, but he still maintained his composure. Waiting for the outcome. After she fell away from his leg from being kick shewed away Antwan walked into his place and slammed the door shut behind him. Sariah stayed on the ground a bit sobbing and uttering his name.

A few minutes dragged out before an Uber came to retrieve her and her belongings. Before the ride got there Antwan, came out and picked her up before the Uber's arrival. Then he escorted her to the car as if he was the perfect gentleman and kissed her on the forehead like he was the last don or something.

"What the fuck!?" Semaj exclaimed.

This nigga had pure nerve and he was gonna serve justice on him tonight. Whether it be from his #38 snub nose special or his fists, the nigga was gonna get his issue tonight.

Once the Uber pulled off Semaj begin to load up his weapon. Five shells for every round he was thinking about emptying on this bitch nigga. Then he sat and waited. Time always moved slowly when an event in his life was getting ready to be ominous. It was now or never he said to himself. He was about to get out when Antwan's front door opened. He came out with an attractive woman closely by his side.

the ASUNDER *Story*... PART ONE: ENTER THE FIRE

"Look at this nigga!" he expressed.

That explains everything. Oh, now he was really going to give it to him. The two of them walked away from the house passing a blunt back and forth to each other, oblivious to what was about to happen to them. Once they turned the corner, he waited a few more minutes before they were good and gone to his liking. He put on his black ski mask and Scully, got out his car, silently closed the door and approached the house. He heard a dog barking viciously as he homed in on the house. He waited patient on the side of the place. The animal on the inside continued barking as if it couldn't wait to tear into somebody ass. He loved dogs and animals for that matter, but if this mad dog got in his way tonight, he'd put an end to it as well.

Suddenly, he heard laughter and conversation coming from around the corner. The couple still unaware of his presence, got to the front of the door never noticing him come from the side of the house. Antwan came in and tried silencing his dog, which was a blue pit-bull mastiff the size of a baby pony. He turned around to say something to his girlfriend who was standing there idly and seen him.

He abruptly pulled down the child proof gate and the animal sprung into attack mode. Semaj lifted the revolver and

the ASUNDER Story...PART ONE: ENTER THE FIRE

pulled the trigger blowing the dogs head halfway across the room. The animal fell to the ground instantly. He'd say a prayer for the poor fella. The gun went off so loudly that you couldn't hear the girl screaming. Antwan stood for a moment of shock and silence as his dog laid on the ground twitching like a bad dream.

Finally coming to reality, he turned around and ran for the back door. He fired another round at the back of his leg. The impact of the bullet spun him around and he went down as well. Now the woman was still standing there screaming, while to shocked to move. This irritated the fuck out of him because it was this bitch that caused his sister to get played.

"Shut the fuck up. You dumb bitch!" he yelled at her and flashed the revolver on her. She immediately went down to a whimper.

"Now get the fuck over there by your man and lay down."

The woman stood there for a few seconds frozen in fear.

"Bitch did you hear me!" he yelled at her and flashed his weapon again.

She did as she was told and laid beside Antwan slightly whimpering.

"Now where is the shit my nigga!" he said speaking with

the ASUNDER *Story*...PART ONE: ENTER THE FIRE

a strange accent. Antwan tried to say something, but he was in and out of consciousness, his words slurring.

He walked over to the couple and snatched the girl up so she could maneuver him through the house. She was still softly whining and that wasn't gonna get him anywhere.

"Bitch if I gotta tell you to be quiet again I'm gonna smoke your boots, you hear me!" he screamed.

She did the best she could. And walked him up the stairs, leading the way. He looked over the banister checking on Antwan, who seemed to be unconscious or dead. He hoped it was the latter.

When they got upstairs, she took them to the master bedroom and went straight to the closet. She searched for a brief minute, as Semaj played her close. Eventually she came out with a safe.

"Now open it up." He said calmly. She did as she was asked and accomplished nothing.

"I-I don't know the code sir." She expressed in a shaky voice.

"Well let's go downstairs and wake yo nigga ass up...come on!" he exclaimed.

She led the way down the stairs and went over to Antwan. She tried asking him the code, but he wasn't

the ASUNDER *Story*... PART ONE: ENTER THE FIRE

responding. So, he made her check his pulse to see if the nigga was still breathing. She did as she was told and checked his pulse. She turned around gave him a head nod. Okay he was still alive then. He hadn't planned on killing him, so he was good with that. Then he told her to take the safe to the door and go back and lay beside Antwan.

"I'ma leave and count to ten...if you get up before I get to ten that's yo ass honey, no bullshit."

He began his countdown while heading out the door. Days later Antwan was in the hospital recovering from his wound. Sariah stayed in visitation the entire time he spent there crying. Semaj tried consoling his sister, but she hated him at that moment. In her heart of hearts, she believed he was behind Antwan's dilemma. It was too ironic that he was shot the night of their disagreement. And she found out later that their mother had contacted her brother the night of the ordeal. She just knew her brother had something to do with it.

"Wake up young nigga it's count time!" G.S. said waking him up.

Freedom woke up almost in a stupor. His head was still spinning, but nowhere near what it was spinning like before he fell into that deep sleep. Freedom went to the sink and threw some water on his face, still infuriated with G.S. for not telling him what he had smoked. It was nothing though because payback is a bitch.

Count time was underway and Ms. Golden walked by the door and smiled at G.S. like they had some type of secret between them. Freedom looked at her stunning beauty and smiled at her as well. She just walked away shaking her head.

"Fuck you then." He said under his breath. Somehow GS still heard him.

"Nah young gangsta, listen you wanna get your man off?" he asked him.

"Nigga I don't want shit from you." Freedom expressed slightly angry still.

"Hold up young G, I gotta proposal for you...seriously."

Freedom stared at him not saying a word waiting for GS to make his proposal.

"Ayight, listen if you can get somebody to make this call for me, I'll see if I can get you some time with the Golden girl...personal time."

Now the old nigga was trying to keep the room cordial. That was a decent proposal, but what was the chances of that? COs just don't do things with random guys who just came on the soil. Had to be some bullshit. And he already tricked him into smoking some dumb ass shit. He didn't trust it.

the ASUNDER Story...PART ONE: ENTER THE FIRE

"Old gangsta you just tricked me into smoking some spice...you think I believe anything that comes outta your mouth?"

"I tell you what after count clears you stay in here and I'ma have Ms. Golden come to the room and get you right...so don't leave the room." GS said nonchalantly.

This was something that could possibly happen.

"Now what am I supposed to be doing for you to make this supposedly happen?" he asked GS full of dubiety in his tone.

"All I need you to do is make a phone call to the Big Apple...simple as that...and just to let you know that I meant no harm from earlier I'm gonna get you right before you make the call...you can have the Golden girl for a few minutes...and a few minutes is all your gonna need...so can I trust you to make the call?"

"Damn right we can definitely make that happen... so you mean to tell me I'm gonna get some pussy on my first week? That's wus up!" Freedom exclaimed.

"Whoa my nigga I didn't say you was gonna get some ass...I just said she was gonna take care of a quick favor for you...now you gonna be the only nigga in here that will get this opportunity...so don't go fuckin this up ayight." GS said a bit

the ASUNDER Story... PART ONE: ENTER THE FIRE

annoyed.

"That's what's really good." Freedom commented sounding like a big kid.

Count cleared and Freedom stayed where he was. GS left the room soon after the doors opened. This was really getting ready to happen. And who knows once the door close it was no telling what was going to happen. GS couldn't stop nothing once that door closed. He smirked at the possibilities. It only took a few minutes before Ms. Golden popped up at his cell door, looking like she had a divine purpose to serve him.

She stood at the door as if she wasn't coming in. Then she whispered some words to him. It seems like she said pull it out. Freedom sat there a bit baffled at the gesture. This is some bullshit he thought. She wasn't coming in the cell. So, GS tricked him again. The situation was what it was though. He walked up to the door and whispered something to her.

"Listen I dunno what the deal is but I can't just pull my shit out while you stand there and look...so how bout we get together on our time?"

She looked puzzled and turned around to see whatever.

"You know what little boy, you gotta lot to learn and when you figure it out, we can probably talk about it." She mentioned to him. Then she turned and surveyed her surroundings again.

"What you mean little boy...boo I'ma grown ass man and since you think I'ma boy put your hands in your back pocket and carry yo ass." He expressed.

She snickered at his comment, showing them pretty pearls off in her mouth. Not being able to contain himself he smiled back at her.

"I tell you what, Semaj we'll talk later, but I will let you know when the time is right." She smiled again and left away from his door.

Okay, the future was set in motion, well at least it appeared to be in his mind. He smiled to himself and began thinking things over. Now soon as Ms. Golden left the door GS was opening the cell door. He also had this sardonic smirk on his face. Freedom was slightly irritated.

"So, you good young gangsta?" he asked Freedom.

"Yeah, GS we fine my man she enjoyed the show." He said halfhearted lying.

"Okay so I need you to make that phone call this evening, and if everything goes well you can maybe get another visit from the Golden girl, ya dig."

Freedom didn't respond he just shook his head knowing

that he had already made his own plans for the Golden girl. He got up and left the cell and went out into the recreation room. He sat amongst his peers and assessed the dayroom. This was his playground for a while, and he was going to take full advantage of it. GS was a manipulating snake and he needed to get the fuck away from him. It was a matter of time before shit just went sideways and GS had a lot more experience in this pothole.

While deep in his thoughts Fuzzy walked up to him and asked him if he could speak to him in his cell briefly. Freedom didn't like the idea, but if he was going to survive in this place then he might just need to see what the old school wanted to talk to him about. Fuzzy's room was upstairs. Once they got to his room he ushered Freedom to his chair, which was well cushioned from the seat to the back support. Then he walked over to the door window and put up the curtain. Freedom remained cool. He felt that whatever Fuzzy was about to do he could handle himself, at least he hoped he could. Fuzzy went to the footlocker and opened it up. He pulled out a wooden box, that had a security lock on it. He told Freedom to turn on the TV while he was putting in the security code. He did as he was asked while keeping a hawk's eye on the older man. After opening the box, he passed it to Freedom, who stared at the

the ASUNDER Story... PART ONE: ENTER THE FIRE

box as if it were some poisonous snakes. As if reading his mind he said to Freedom,

"That's your weapon in this bitch young gangsta. Ya dig?"

Freedom didn't say anything he just stared at the shanks as if they were volatile and about to jump out the box.

"You might not ever use them, but jealousy, lust, envy, and greed cause a muthafucka to be on some spiteful shit in here."

Freedom picked out the smallest one he could see and eagerly passed the box back to Fuzzy. Then he went to put the shank in his pocket. Fuzzy took the box away from him and put it back in the locker. The weapon was sticking out his pocket like a stupid sore thumb

"Nah young gangsta you can't just put it in your pocket all willy nilly...put that shit in your sock or something, tighten up." Fuzzy expressed icy than a glacier.

Freedom dapped him up, said nothing and left the room as fast as he'd came in there. He was glad to get out of there with the man. To him Fuzzy was like a warm breeze of death quiet, and his etiquette was vicious, to mean for him to be in company with.

the ASUNDER Story... PART ONE: ENTER THE FIRE

As he was leaving from the top tier, he passed Ms. Golden, who was making her mall rounds.

"Do you like white woman?" she asked him flirtatiously.

He seemed to be thrown off guard by the question, but wittiness was his greatest attribute he responded, "Do you like black snakes?"

"Fact's I do, as long as my gardens been in need of something devilish." She commented just as witty.

Wow he thought she was gonna be his Eve and he was gonna have her committing all types of ungodly sins.

"I'm not Lucifer but boo I promise I can make you feel like every bite of that apple was worth biting into." He said almost in a whisper.

"Ohh daddy now I just might let you play in my garden then... maybe this weekend."

His cock immediately begins rising like a Phoenix sun. Seeing that caused her to step off smooth criminal Mike Jackson.

He went downstairs to make that call for GS. He must make this exclusive phone call and maybe, just maybe he could do what GS said he couldn't do to this officer. Shit, the way she had just talked to him he probably could have her just the way he wanted at any time.

the ASUNDER Story... PART ONE: ENTER THE FIRE

The clock read 8:57 AM...a bit past the time he normally calls. His family usually is out the house around 8 o'clock. He needed to get through this morning and be done with the call for GS, this call was going to be a game changer. He called home and was able to get through to his brother.

"What's up big bro, how're you?" Daniel asked him enthusiastically.

"I'm good, I just need you to make an important phone call for a friend of mine." Semaj said.

"Well, is it long distance...? Cus you know how mom be acting bout long distance phone calls."

"I dunno bro if it's long distance, he just needs me to make an important phone call." He lied. GS needed to call the Big Apple and he wasn't going to let his mom get in the way of that. Especially knowing that Ms. Golden was potentially going to be with him in the future.

"Listen big bro I can do it for him this time, but mom says the phone is only for you...well you know how mom is?"

"Well, I appreciate that bro, he really needs to get through to his family." Semaj expressed slyly. He called for GS to the phone and put him through. He talked roughly about 10 minutes and passed the phone back to Freedom. He looked at him and threw him a thumbs up. Okay his part was done, now

the ASUNDER *Story*... PART ONE: ENTER THE FIRE

Ms. Golden was on his menu.

"Hey brother who was that guy?" Daniel asked Semaj.

"Why? What's the problem? Were you listening to him?" Semaj asked him a bit indignant.

"No, I wasn't listening to his phone call I just tried to see if he had given you back the phone and I overheard him and some woman saying that she sent the $5000 dollars." Daniel shot back.

"Okay bro, I got you, no problem...I didn't mean to sound like I was attacking you...thanks anyway for that."

"Okay not a problem, but please try not to make it a habit calling people for other folks...I mean seriously I don't think anyone getting $5000 dollars sent to them are in need of a serious phone call."

"Again, bro okay, I get it...um so I'ma call you later on." He sighed and before his brother could say anything else he hung up the line.

He strolled over to the table where GS and Fuzzy were sitting playing what looked like an intense chess game. Suddenly Fuzzy checkmated GS with a smile.

"Dammit old nigga you make me sick...I had yo old ass." GS exclaimed.

"You know why you can't beat me GS, cus you a dressed-up trash can...you look good around here beating up on these rookies but when you call me out, I take out the trash on yo bum ass game."

"Play one more game old nigga." GS sounded upset.

"You know you already owe me $150 young man don't keep running up the coins...cus you can't beat me."

"Goddamn Fuzzy why don't you tell the whole got'damn building how much I owe you." He exclaimed.

"GS, I really don't give a damn how mad you are nigga, you called out the wrong muthafucka and you can't deal with it...so put up or get up." Fuzzy said calmly but sternly.

"Yeah, alright old gangsta I lose this game I'm done...just know this, every dog has it's day...eventually I'ma beat you down like you stole something from me."

They set up the chess pieces and went to war. Freedom watched them play a little before GS asked him about Ms. Golden. He mentioned that he seen her, but it wasn't nothing special. GS looked at him with a sinical look on his face as if he knew other than. Freedom looked away from him and stared off as if ignoring GS.

Fuzzy was watching him from the corner of his eye.

"Yo Freedom you gotta be about your business around here...this is what goes on around here...hustle, hustle, hustle hard and only close one eye when it's lock up time... you dig Freedom?"

"Yeah, Fuzzy I dig it." He mentioned. GS looked at him as if he envied his youth and said something that would resonate in his mind for the rest of his life.

"Freedom loyalty is greater than anything in this world. Love is honored by respect. Don't lose any of those qualities and you'll go to the grave with the same power as Christ had when he came from the grave on the third day." Freedom just sat there in silence looking into space.

The weekend was here. Freedom was anxious and tense. Wanting someone with this kind of yearning never felt so compelling when he was home. He was a pro in the bed, but it's been 18 long months since he'd last performed and put on for a woman.

C/O Ms. Golden was just as nervous. She had to be he thought. This morning in the chow hall she didn't say one word to him or GS. Maybe she was evading the whole ordeal they had set up over the week. That would mean GS set him up for failure. His mom always told him never to trust man, for man wasn't God. And when God spoke to man's heart, he might not show up when one expected, but he was always right on time. That's how God worked and of course man was nothing like the

the ASUNDER *Story*... PART ONE: ENTER THE FIRE

most high.

"Damn this bitch and nigga prolly is playing me and for what...they both needed me." He said to no one while lying on his rack.

GS was nowhere to be found and he kind of was hoping that he was hoping that he could bring confirmation to the restless, maybe eased the troubled waters in his head. It wasn't GS fault that she was eluding him. Even though he acted like he controlled her every move she made the final call, bottom line.

He needed a nap. Maybe she'd come by tonight or Sunday. GS did say this weekend. It was barely Saturday noonish. He would have a catnap and of course that would ease some of the tension he was experiencing. Then he'd wake up to the deliciousness of Ms. Golden. That would be phenomenal.

Freedom was sound asleep when he felt the warmth and wetness of her lips fully take down his head and shaft. What was happening had to be surreal. He was dreaming. To be sure of the moment he gently caressed her hair. That gesture alone caused her to turn up the experience. Each time she'd journey up and down his length she'd look seductively into the haziness of his brown eyes. Her tongue played lustfully with the slit of his tip. She moaned softly encouraging him to reach his climax and reluctantly he did. She got up, went to the sink, gargled some water in her mouth and spit it in the toilet. Before she left the cell, she tuned and blew him a kiss. Then she was gone. He was mesmerized.

After getting his thoughts in order, he went to the sink and washed himself off. He smiled at his reflection in the Steele mirror.

"You the man...I said you the man." He mentioned, feeling his ego swell to the gods.

Just as he was finishing up GS popped up in the door with a smug facial expression, which blew Freedom making him very uncomfortable.

"Did she handle the business young gangsta?" GS asked him cool like.

"She was decent." He said nonchalantly. He was lying, she was more than decent, in fact that was the best head quicky he had in his life.

"Yeah, I bet she was more than decent." GS commented reading right through him like always.

Freedom ignored him and lied down. Just as he was getting relaxed someone knocked on the cell door. GS peeked out the door window, then opened it up. A shabby looking white guy came in looking googly eyed. He wanted something but seemed to loss for words. GS looked from him to Freedom as he chuckled to himself. Finally, after what seemed like forever the man said,

"I want some more."

GS held out his hand wiggling his fingers as if he was playing cat and mouse with whatever the man wanted, and he possessed. He gave GS a fifty-dollar bill. Freedom was taken aback. He never thought he'd see real dead presidents in prison. He'd heard rumors and stories as well as watched movies, but he didn't believe any of the hype until now.

GS walked over to the dresser: picked up a roll-on deodorant, opened the top and took out the roll-on ball after a bit of a struggle and retrieved what looked like some white crystals. It looked like meth. The guy walked over to him and picked out three small baggies. After the transaction the man was gone just as fast as he'd come in. GS fixed the roll-on and put it back on the shelf with the rest of his cosmetic city. All those cosmetics made quite the decoy.

Then GS pulled out a neat wad of money and counted it. He counted $750 dollars in Freedom's face as if it was common to him. Then he took out $150 dollars for Fuzzy's and his chest match, earlier that week. He put the rest of his money in his pocket and left out the cell as arrogantly and dignified as he could. Freedom wanted to ask him how he could get paid in

the **ASUNDER** *Story*... **PART ONE: ENTER THE FIRE**

full as well but thought against it. That would only add gas to his gassed-up ego. He left the room a few minutes after GS and went to Fuzzy's cell. He wasn't there. His celli told him he was on the rec-yard.

He went to the yard in search for the old school. He found him on the weight pit going extremely hard. Freedom wasn't interested with the workout regimen. He had a solid physique too. He apparently was blessed with the benefits of good genes along with good eating. He was natural. Fuzzy might want to test his physical attributes and put him under a weight bench.

"Damn!" he said in his head. Regardless of the weight pile, he had to talk to him. If it meant working-out to get the ball rolling, fuck it he'd be pumping some iron this morning.

Fuzzy came from under the incline bench, wiped off his forehead and spotted Freedom standing idly by.

"What's good with you young gangsta?" he asked Freedom.

"I'm good Fuzzy... I actually wanted to speak with you about something."

"Ayo Fuzzy it's your turn under the bench big fam you know we super setting." His workout partner exclaimed.

"Go ahead Jimbob, I'ma catch you on the back set... lemme talk to youngen...check the trap." Fuzzy said.

They walked off, taking a spin around the track. The yard was huge, supposedly a two-mile radius. Freedom didn't want to hold him up with his business. He hoped to get everything out in one lap.

"Ayo I'm tryna get me some money... I mean I got my family holding me down, but if I could get my own paper that would help my peoples out." Freedom announced setting the tone.

"Freedom it's money all this bitch... you got every kinda drug in here...you got every kinda addict. You got pussy in that can make you money. It's money in the kitchen...shit you can even lake some loot working out...so when you say you tryna get some money you have to be more specific."

"Alright, I'm tryna get a mule...someone to bring me the pack preferably a female." Freedom proclaimed with Ms. Golden in mind.

"Well first lemme say a mule can be anybody...I prefer a female too, but I'll take it any way I can...you gotta. You can't be picky about who's bringin in the shit, as long as ya'll have an understanding on who gets what."

"GS seems to have all types of ways to get shit in."

the ASUNDER *Story*... PART ONE: ENTER THE FIRE

"Well, first of all Freedom you can't worry about what the next man is doing... you gotta be about you... GS been in the game for years, not once can I recall him being picky about who his mule was"

"I guess your right on that part Fuzzy." He commented.

"You guess I'm right...Freedom if you wanna get some money, up here can get it. You ain't got time to be sitting around worrying who bringin in the product...you dig me."

"I got you Fuzz."

Fuzzy continued, "Now what's the purpose for making this money."

"Well, you already know, so I can stay fly and fresh as well as comfortable."

"Freedom you got the wrong idea...see if all you wanna do is stay fly, fresh and comfortable you'll have the shortest run-in penitentiary history. These whities ain't green beans. They'll be on you like dog shit unexpected on the bottom of your shoes...then when they catch you, they'll persecute you like Jesus, hang you high so we can bear witness to your downfall...now what's your purpose for making money?"

"Okay Fuzzy my lil brother wants to become a fashion designer...he goes to school in LIU in Brooklyn. He's majoring in business and fashion...he has two years left before graduating...I want to help him start up his clothing empire. I don't want him to have to worry about how he's gonna get money or go to a bank that's gonna pimp the shit outta him...my lil bro help's me out I just wanna be able to give back."

"Now you gotta goal in mind...see if you tryna meet this goal you ain't gonna let nothing or nobody hinder you...going back to what I said you don't care who's helping you get that money as long as you are getting that money you dig."

"That's wus good Fuzzy...so how we gonna move on the situation?" Freedom responded.

"I'ma holla at a few people and see wus up and get wit you okay my nigga." Freedom continued his stroll around the track. The rec yard was so grand, so many inmates in their own world. A whistle blew for gate break. He decided to go back in, he did what he came out here to do. He had his own plan in mind and whatever Fuzzy was going to do for him, he would be his backup plan. C/O Golden was going to be his initial plan A. He knew that was going to cause some problems between him and GS, but like he thought this morning pussy didn't belong to only woman and maybe God and then when God acted like he owned the pussy she'd just turn to the garden snake and commit ungodly sins. Freedom laughed at his thoughts.

the ASUNDER *Story...* PART ONE: ENTER THE FIRE

GS had a visit, which seemed to have been a good one. When he came to the cell, he took out aa couple of balloons from out the crack of his ass. Freedom was looking at him closely while listening to the Jp5 he had let him use. GS was at the table taking care of his business. Freedom thought to himself that for a man who claimed he was an entrepreneur he certainly had his hand in a lot of the drug trade.

Freedom was in a zone when GS turned around and asked him told him to come here. He took the headphones off and went over to the table. GS passed him a razor and a block of some cocaine. Freedom wasn't really a drug dealer, but he knew that the block that in front of him was at least a quarter ounce.

"Freedom that is about a quarter ounce and two grams...cut me off twenty dime pieces, five twenty pieces, and six fifty blocks...do you know how to eyeball work?"

"Yeah, I can hook it up for you." Freedom said fronting. He didn't want GS to think he was incompetent when it came to the matter at hand.

"You sure?" GS said inquisitively.

"My man I told you I got this no problem." Freedom responded coolly.

GS grabbed the remote and turned the television to BET,

the ASUNDER *Story*...PART ONE: ENTER THE FIRE

then he put the curtain up in the window. He came back to the table and broke open the other balloon and poured out some off-white caps. He reached under the table and took out a porcelain plate. He opened the baggie and dumped the caps onto the plate. He opened two of the caps and made two reasonable size lines on the plate. He told Freedom he could make at least twenty dollars of each one of those lines, street money. He had at least 30 caps which meant he was looking at $1200-$1300 dollars give or take. After they were done chopping and bagging GS grabbed all the utensils and put them in their proper places. Then he took 20 caps of the heroine and all the cocaine and put it in between his butt cheeks. After making sure everything was done, he checked the cell one more time for flaws then he exited the room.

Freedom put the headphones back on and laid back on his bunk thinking to himself how he was going to get paid. Although he had Ms. Golden in mind, he still had to be leery of GS.

His mind was mellowing out when someone knocked on his cell door. He couldn't hear their knock beyond the loud music in his ears. She let herself in and closed the door behind her. She walked up to him and touched him on the shoulder.

Freedom jumped up off guard startled. He took off the

the ASUNDER Story... PART ONE: ENTER THE FIRE

headphones and asked her what was up. She told him that she wanted to meet him in the laundry room tonight at 6 o'clock. He had to move with the night traffic when the nightly activities got underway. He didn't know exactly where the building was. She gave him a quick run-down on the building locale because she needed to get out of the cell. Then she told him about the door on the right side was going to be opened and to come in and close it behind him. He protested but before he could get anything out of his mouth she was gone like a light wind.

    Count time was less than 15 minutes away, Freedom had dosed off to sleep. He had a dream that he was having sex with Angelón in the laundry room he hadn't seen yet. He had her bent over a table banging her voluptuous pretty round ass from behind and enjoying every bit of her moans. She had her lovely long sparkling orange locks swaying down the dip in the center of her back. She was chanting his name and right before he was about to release his nut deep into her wombs, the door to the laundry room burst open like hells gates. It was C/O Miles and GS. Freedom came out of her and tried pulling up his pants just as GS rocked him square in the face sending him into a washing machine totally across the room.

    After Freedom was unconscious GS went over to C/O

the ASUNDER *Story*...PART ONE: ENTER THE FIRE

Miles and Ms. Golden who was being held down against her will. He stood over her and asked her,

"Who the fuck told you to give my pussy away!" GS shouted in her face spittle flying everywhere like mad drool.

"Yeah, who the hell told you to give GS's pussy away you slut!" C/O Miles exclaimed hollering as well.

She tried to speak but GS bent down and smacked the taste and words out of her mouth. She was screaming for Freedom, but he was out like an 'off' switch. She continued calling for him until he was really coming out of a good dream gone nightmare, into the realization of Fuzzy shaking him to get up.

"Yo, yo wus good Fuzzy?!" He complained half wake.

"Look here young buck they got GS...that's all I know at the moment!" Fuzzy said hysterically.

"Damn..." seemed to be the only word he could muster.

"I peeped him coming outta building 4 with a rack of C/O's in tow and they escorted my guy to the seg building...and guess who was with them officer's, Ms. Golden girl...like I told this nigga this bitch was up to something, but he always told me I'm thinking too much about nothing."

"Yo this shit crazy old gangsta." Freedom said without any emotions. Then Fuzzy told him that it was almost time for

the ASUNDER *Story*... PART ONE: ENTER THE FIRE

count and that he had to get back to his cell. Next, he told him that when count cleared, he'd back down to his cell to help him with all paraphernalia that might get him or his celli some type of heavy scrutinization. Then he left the cell.

Freedom got up and went to the door and looked out of his window. An officer was walking by looking in rooms then closing and locking the cell doors. Freedom did him the honors and closed his door himself. The officer got by his door looked in at the cell door number, jotted down his door number and scurried off. Freedom was a bit distraught he just knew GS was too much of a thinker to be caught off guard by a guard who he implied wasn't shit; moreover, what kind of involvement could Ms. Golden possibly have in the entire ordeal. This bitch was playing devil's advocate.

Then something that registered in his deepest wits was shit happens to the best of them. He was wondering how GS got caught up. It just wasn't a normal situation, smelling really fishy like. What he couldn't understand was why GS took so much shit out of the room that day. Someone had to have set him up, that's a strong possibility. He wondered to himself if he should still go over to the laundry room. Although he still wanted to have her could he take that risk? Then it dawned on him what Fuzzy had told him about Ms. Golden coming out of

the ASUNDER Story... PART ONE: ENTER THE FIRE

the building with the entourage of officers. She could be some type of federal officer setting niggas up in this joint or something. Who knew with all these thoughts going on in his head, he still wanted to try his hand but, could he take that chance?" She could at least clarify things for him. Or maybe have him caught up too.

"Damn Ms. Golden who the fuck are you?" he muttered thinking out loud.

He heard a whistle being blown very loudly signaling count time. The C/O's walked pass his door and one of them tapped it with a pen. Then he shot his thumb up for Freedom to stand up. He stood up taking his everlasting time. The next officer that passed his door was black, matter of fact he was so black he appeared purple. He hadn't seen any black Officer's on this spread since he'd arrived here. Freedom thought to himself that the C/O was an Uncle Tom. He had to be because a brother who was walking around with the man's badge of honor oppressing people of the same ethnicity was a porch monkey, plain and simple. After count cleared, he would go to Fuzzy's cell and see what was going on with GS. Then he would wait for the moment of truth with Ms. Golden and see what the deal was with her.

After count cleared Freedom didn't have the chance to

the ASUNDER *Story*...PART ONE: ENTER THE FIRE

go up to Fuzzy's room. He was knocking on his door as if he was the ops or some goddamn body. He opened his door and let him in. Fuzzy must've already knew the drill on what to do just in case something like this ever happened because he grabbed all of GS's stash spots like it was regular routine. Then he put all the paraphernalia in his big fur down coat.

"Be cool young gangsta and whatever they ask you, you don't know nothing." Fuzzy exclaimed and then he walked out the door as if he was making a grand finale exit.

Soon after Fuzzy left his room chow was being announced through the loudspeakers and the night was getting ready to begin. He put on his best state blues and a fresh white tee. Then he dabbed on some of GS's exclusive oil. He was sure he wouldn't mind. On his way out the door he looked at himself in the mirror and smiled. The moment of truth was nigh.

On his way to the chow hall, he seen lil Mike. He hadn't saw him since the first day he arrived on the compound. He asked Freedom how he was doing then in the same sentence he asked him what happened to GS. Freedom had already adapted to the code of the penitentiary: hear no evil, speak no evil, see no evil. He told Lil Mike he didn't know what happened to him and strolled off before Lil Mike could ask him anything else.

When he entered the mess hall someone was yelling his

the ASUNDER Story...PART ONE: ENTER THE FIRE

name, and his government name at that. So, it was obvious that this person knew who he was. Freedom got his tray and went over to the man's table.

"What's good with you homey?" he asked Freedom.

"Shit, I'm coolin'." Was Freedom's response.

Then the man stared at him for a few seconds, which made him somewhat uncomfortable.

Then he said, "Ms. Sloan's class 6th grade!"

Everything hit him at once like an epiphany. "Oh, shit Maxwell Malone!"

"Yeah, my nigga what's been good wit you over the years?"

"Man, I been layin back doin' me for real tho...damn the last time I seen you, no pun taken but you had a snot nose and candlewax all over them ears of yours." Both old acquaintances laughed at this fact.

"No pun intended my gangsta no pun intended." Maxwell expressed still laughing.

A younger dude walked over to their table and gave Maxwell a drawn-out handshake.

"Wus poppin wit you slime?" the man asked Maxwell.

"You know what it be like bloody?" Maxwell replied.

Maxwell introduced Freedom to his homey. He dapped

the ASUNDER *Story*...PART ONE: ENTER THE FIRE

Freedom and slid close to Maxwell and began giving him the run down on something. Freedom couldn't quite make out the conversation, but he did hear GS's name mentioned a few times. After a few more head shakes the guy dapped up Maxwell and left the table. Somebody on the other side of the diner hall was calling for Maxwell, he waved for him to come over to him. It was the same ritual when the guy got to the table. GS's name mentioned once or twice. After this guy left the table Maxwell straight up asked him what happened to his celli. Telling Maxwell about his Bunkie wasn't any of his business. Better kept, if left alone.

Maxwell said, "I was asking you because he was supposed to meet me in here tonight...ain't y'all in the same cell?"

"Yeah, we in the same cell, but I still don't know what happened to him. All I know is that he came from a visit, came into the room for a few minutes, then he bounced. I ain't seen him since." Freedom explained feeling that he gave him too much info, even with that.

"Never mind my nigga. I'll find out what happened to him," calmly Maxwell said.

As they were finishing up their meal, Maxwell told him that he goes by Max-A-Mill now or just Max. Semaj told him that he goes by Freedom. They then dapped each other up and parted ways.

On the way back to the building, Freedom saw Fuzzy coming out of Building Four. He looked upset. He caught up with Fuzzy and asked him what wus up with GS. He told him that everything was good, and that GS wasn't caught up with any drugs.

"He smacked a nigga and the motherfucka went to the control booth and ratted on him," Fuzzy then indicated that GS would be back on the yard, hopefully by Monday.

Six o'clock couldn't take any longer to get here. He kept glancing at the clock on the wall in the cell.

"Damn, this shit takin' forever," Freedom said to himself. Although six o'clock was twenty minutes away, he was restless. He had to keep reassuring himself that he was ready.

The speaker came on and announced for the preparation of the night programs. The moment of clarity was now. He looked at himself in the mirror.

"Ms. Golden, I hope you are worth the hassle," Freedom said to the man in the mirror. He brushed his teeth for the fifth time today. He wanted to make sure his breath was extra fresh. Not that he was gonna kiss her but who knows though. When passion and ecstasy take over your mind and body, you're subject to do anything. "Not I." Freedom uttered to himself.

He dabbed on some of his good cologne oil. The smell wasn't too strong. It was a soft musky smell. It was just right for tonight's festivities.

It was now 5:55 PM. "Here we go. It's game time!" Freedom exclaimed silently to himself before stepping out of the cell and closed his cell's door.

Finally, the programs were getting started. As he was leaving the building, he spotted Max-A-Mill, who was with a bunch of people. He didn't notice Freedom, and he liked it that way. He didn't need to be stopped by anybody.

The catwalk was packed. Everybody going to each's destinations. Freedom saw the laundry building and caught butterflies inside his stomach. He told himself to get it together. Two correctional officers were standing in front of the laundry building conversing.

"Shit!" Freedom expressed angrily. He walked over to the gymnasium and went in. He'd buy some time in here. The gym was enormous. It seemed like everybody on the camp was there. He stood by the door hoping nobody came to bother him. A correctional officer was about to close the door. Freedom stopped him and told him he was about to leave. The

the ASUNDER Story... PART ONE: ENTER THE FIRE

officer told him, before letting him leave that from now on whatever destination he was at, he would have to remain until the programs were done for the night.

The officer knew he was new, because when asked where his night pass was at, not only did he not have one he didn't even know what the officer was talking about. He started to interrogate him some more but was interrupted by a call on his radio. As soon as the officer got on his radio, he walked away from Freedom leaving him by the door. He left out of the door as quickly as possible while the going was good.

He was approaching the laundry building and became nervous again. He gave himself a quick pep talk. There was no one on the boulevard and that was great. Then he came up on the side of the laundry door and turned the knob and the door was slightly ajar already. Thank you, God, he thought.

As he was closing and locking the door a soft hand reached into his hand, pulling him away from the door. He followed her lead. This really was going to happen, he tells himself. A smile quickly sneaked into the corners of his mouth. An eagerness brought on his firm erection. They finally came upon a dimly lit area. Immediately, she blushed at his noticeable manhood standing at attention without shame.

the ASUNDER Story... PART ONE: ENTER THE FIRE

She rubbed his hardness and whispered something that caused his erection to extend even more.

"Not tonight...I asked you to come here to speak with you about something." In utter disbelief, all he could say was, "What!?"

"I need for you to listen to me very carefully, ok?" She waited for him to come to grips with what she just said and did.

Freedom took a heavy sigh looking at her in muddle disbelief. Clearly, he was upset by the sporadic change of event. She played with his head; furthermore, putting him in jeopardy of getting caught. He took a great risk tonight and only to be cut short of the moment.

"Are you aware of the man you're occupying the cell with?" She asked. He played naive when he replied.

"Who? GS?"

"Yes, him."

"Look Mrs. Golden, I didn't risk going through all the chaos and ruckus I went through tonight to come here and talk about a nigga I barely even know," he said confirming his indignation. It was obviously written all over his face.

"I know you didn't...but if you don't hear it from me now, you'll regret the fact that I didn't say anything to you

61

the ASUNDER Story... PART ONE: ENTER THE FIRE

about him at all." She says calmly allowing her eyes to befriend his eyes and trust.

Freedom deeply exhaled leaning against one of the folding tables waiting to hear the dirty laundry she was about to air on GS.

The minutes began to intensify as she continued her spiel about GS's morale, which seem to personify a mastermind. She spoke of him as if he was a spawn brought from the depts of Haiti with legions close by his majesty. He could give a damn though. GS. was a man that took a piss and shit the same way he did. Hell, whatever GS ate didn't make him shit either. It seemed to him that she feared GS. That seemed even more bizarre considering the lusty infatuation he witnessed between her and GS.

If her purpose was to help him beware of the goon, then why is she involved with him? Her motive wasn't yet obvious. Freedom was confused. He hadn't been in the penitentiary a good two weeks and already the allure of drama was beckoning at him. He didn't need the headache, nor did he want to get involved with two lovers' quarrel.

"Umm, listen up shorty. I do appreciate the revelation, but where's the door so I can carry my ass outta here?" The look on Freedom's face was confirmation if looks could kill, Ms.

the ASUNDER *Story*... PART ONE: ENTER THE FIRE

Golden would be mutilated, dismembered, and thrown out in tomorrow's trash. "I ain't got time to be dealing with this shit and ..."

Ms. Golden quickly cupped Freedom's face kissing him immediately quieting his dispute. Her kiss was warm and seductive. Almost waking up his mummified dick. No sooner than she kissed him, Freedom pulled her away from him then looked into her eyes not knowing exactly what to read in them.

"Yo, Ms. Golden...Umm, what I mean is what's up with you?"

"It's complicated Freedom. I...I like you. I really do but we have to tread lightly. Especially given the fact that I'm an offi..."

"Shhh..." he motioned for her silence. Someone was unlocking the door. She heard the keys and door both being fumbled with too.

"Damn!" She expressed anxiously.

"What now?" he asked her nervously.

"Stay put," she motioned with her pointed forefinger. Then she exited the dark room leaving him alone. Freedom's heart was galloping like a horse at the derby race.

Once she was gone from the small room, she went to the door. She turned her radio back on so it wouldn't look suspicious or worse...forgetting to turn it back on all together.

Freedom could hear the radio's static and the scratchy voices over her radio. Then he heard her talking to another officer. Their conversation wasn't audible enough for him to make out what they were discussing. His heart continued pounding loudly in his ears. Sweat began trickling down his forehead and a reminder of his dream replayed back in his mind.

Damn, I should've listened to my dream, he told himself furiously. Soon after, there was utter silence a few minutes later. He impatiently waited in the still of the darkness wondering where Ms. Golden went and when will she return? Finally, he heard the quick taps of boots rushing toward the room he was in. She appeared and turned the lights back on. She grabbed him, pulling him close and kissed him again while raising one hand to slip the light switch back off and escorted him through the darkness never bumping into anything. Freedom took mental notes of that. After they reached the door, she stopped and looked over at him.

"Freedom, I'm a corrections officer. I need you to remember that in the eyes of the public. You know what I mean?"

Freedom tilted his head sideways looking at her snidely, "I

the ASUNDER Story... PART ONE: ENTER THE FIRE

know this shorty. I ain't green to the game." His voice radiated disgust with the idea of her thinking he was slow let alone careless. When, she seemed to be moving reckless.

Slowly Ms. Golden opened the door and peeked out. Then she told him to leave out. He stepped out and looked around briefly then slid off quiet as kept.

On the way back to the building, he began to wonder if she was worth the trouble. She was sexy no doubt, but she was straight up bold as shit. That's what Freedom was attracted to. Her willingness was a turn on as well as hands down irresistible. However, the drama he would be subjected to if they were found out would undoubtingly prove to be brutal. So, they must make sure G.S. did not catch wind of what Ms. Golden and he were doing behind his back. That was the problem now overwhelming his mind.

Their first rendezvous was orchestrated by the very person who claimed no one would have her body but him. He would prove that to be a lie. That was his little head trying to convince him that everything was a go. Ms. Golden told him some pertinent shit about Godfrey. Maybe they were all lies. Perhaps it could've been true. Whatever the case was, he now knew that his cellmate was no joke, and if he got caught slipping, he was...done!

the ASUNDER *Story*... PART ONE: ENTER THE FIRE

After getting back to his cell, he started putting things into perspective. Ms. Golden was on the verge of being his new thing. It was so much they could accomplish together. All he had to do was move accordingly and competition would no longer be his concern. He knew G.S. would fade away but he was not gonna leave easily as a smooth summer breeze.

She depicted G.S. as a one-man militia. Fresh out Kuwait and that was dangerous. When it was all said and done, the question that would be hovering was simple. 'Could he survive and come out unscathed?'

"Damn!" he uttered out loud.

Tonight, he was alone, but the walls seemed to be whispering. G.S. was a serious force to be reckoned with and all signs seem to point to that. He never had to prepare for anything. He just responded. His mom's voice resonated in his head with one of the quotes she famously used, *'Fear is false evidence appearing real. Never succumb to what can't be proven.'*

At this moment, GS was Ms. Golden's fears and not his. He smirked at the wisdom of a wise woman.

"I got this," he said calmly before closing his eyes letting sleep engulf his body.

PART II

the ASUNDER *Story*...PART ONE: ENTER THE FIRE

Chapter 2

the ASUNDER Story...PART ONE: ENTER THE FIRE

I Can Feel It in The Air

The weekend was over too fast. GS was released from segregation Monday morning. He mentioned to Freedom that he felt rejuvenated and needed that. Freedom thought to himself that he wasn't gone but two days. Freedom felt partly anew as well. He'd almost accomplished what GS claimed no one could do to Ms. Golden but him. He supposedly knew exclusive gossip about GS. She talked about him intensely without pause. In fact, with Diamond's clarity. She said he was egotistical and selfish too. And those character flaws were minor on the scale of his wicked soul. He really didn't know anything about GS, nor could he fully trust Ms. Golden, but he knew one thing for sure and two things for certain was that GS was selfish. That seemed to be right so far Saturday afternoon, he had helped him chop and bag up half of his product he didn't offer him jack shit either. Needless to say, *thanks for nothing*.

GS seemed very enigmatic in totality. He just hoped he was prepared when shit hits the fan and blow him away. GS attended anger management classes on Mondays and Wednesdays. So, for the first few hours of the morning Freedom was alone. GS told him that he could watch his flat

the ASUNDER *Story*...PART ONE: ENTER THE FIRE

(19"TV) which GS seemed to be the only one with of such proportion. That was the exception for the rich and infamous. He decided against watching GS's TV because if something happened to it, he'd be the blame. Instead, Freedom opted to listen to his JP5 player until he got his and maybe that was already too risky. He got himself together; put on some sweatpants and went to the recreation yard.

    It was roughly past 8 o'clock in the morning but the yard was packed with convicts and inmates. Convicts were what Fuzzy referred to everyone that were old gangstas. They were the niggas who supposedly were the heartbeat in the concrete jungle. Inmates were the young punks pushin' these watered-down gangs beating themselves up, while the man stayed pushin' dick in them. Freedom snickered to himself thinking on the old man's penial sage.

    He began his stroll around the track. He spotted Max-A-Mill again surrounded with massive niggas. He wondered what his position was in the Blood Nation. It had to be a heavy status and not because the men were always in his shadow. When GS came back to the cell this morning, the first person's name he mentioned was Max-A-Mill. Him speaking your name first thing in the morning spoke volumes of who you were, considering that he was that nigga.

the ASUNDER *Story*... PART ONE: ENTER THE FIRE

As he was walking by Max saw him and yelled for him to come over to where they were. Freedom didn't like being interrupted from the mission at hand. Right now, Max-A-Mill was disturbing his morning route. It couldn't hurt shit, though. It might be something he needed to hear or know.

"What's up Free?" Max asked him.

"Ain't shit. What's hood wit' you, my nigga?" Freedom retorted cool and smooth.

"You already know. Look though, I wanna talk to you 'bout some things. For real it's been a while, but you still seem like the same Gee that I've always knew you as."

"However, brief..." Freedom's response cut and dry.

Max-A-Mill and Freedom stepped off in conversation. Max caught him up on things including his status. He'd recently became a three-star general and represented O.M.G.B. (Official Money Gettin' Blood).

He told Freedom that his big homie Five, who was an OG let him start up his own set. Everything still went through Five. Max had gotten his status he shot and killed a dude who disrespected him and his movement on the streets. He told Freedom that if he wanted to join his set, all he had to do was go through something called a tré-one. He asked Max what that was. Max smiled and asked him if he'd ever been jumped.

the ASUNDER Story... PART ONE: ENTER THE FIRE

He claimed he had been jumped by two niggas. He stressed to Max that he did handle his business regardless.

They reminisced how much he fought in school. They didn't go into detail as to why he fought so much. Max thought that it could've been that he stayed in some freshness and his swagger flaunted in the faces of those who felt threatened by his location. That was the reason why Max fucked with him in school and wanted to deal with him now. Only this time, Max was the big Dawg on campus or at least that's what he thought. They walked and talked a little while longer. Afterwards, Max told him to think about their conversation and get back with him.

Freedom continued his morning stroll along the track. He felt respected, but he didn't necessarily feel that he needed to be in a gang or a movement for that matter. He could stand on his own two and contend with the best of them, both physically and mentally. He thought about how things would benefit him by joining their cause. He didn't need or want protection and he definitely didn't want their problems. To him what came with the life was more than a headache. After pondering on that situation, he could do without the extra attention. At least for now anyway. You could never say never though.

the ASUNDER *Story*...PART ONE: ENTER THE FIRE

He saw Fuzzy working out. He strolled over to the pit. Fuzzy was just putting down some eighty-pound dumbbells. Freedom was impressed. Being in his fifties and looking like he did, said a lot about his diet and workout regimen. He probably wouldn't look fifty if his hair was all the way black. Fuzzy didn't notice Freedom approaching. He called his name. Fuzzy turned around to see who was calling him. He acknowledged him and held up one finger, telling him to hold up a sec. He did another set of curls, dropped the steel on the ground, and gave his workout partner some dap. The young guy kept working out. Fuzzy was cut up from the butt up.

"What's on 'ur mind Freedom?" Fuzzy expressed a bit frazzled.

"Ay yo Fuzz, if somebody owned a home and the homeowner allowed someone to stay there and pay rent, only, can the person paying rent, sometimes eat out of the fridge without him knowing?"

He thought about the question before responding. Then spoke.

"Freedom, on any man's property that's being rented out to another person, unless they allow you to utilize things in their home, it's off limits...Why? Whose house you tryna rent a room in while you're locked up?"

the ASUNDER Story...PART ONE: ENTER THE FIRE

"Well, I don't know if you could or would call it rent. You see the house might be mine if I could convince the homeowner to pack their shit, give 'em a coupla dollars and tell 'em to bounce, move it, sorta like a foreclosure," Freedom jokingly expressed. He was trying to make funny out of a serious situation. Maybe to appease his own guilt.

Fuzzy smirked and said, "If you're down 'wit O.P.P. (Other People's Property) then do what you gotta do."

He wanted to tell Fuzzy where things were going with him and the Golden girl, but Fuzzy was GS's right-hand man, and Ms. Golden was his right-hand man's lady. So, he left that thought in the clouds.

"Freedom, a real man gets his own. God bless the child that has his own...and maybe you must swindle motherfucka's and once you gain what you desired it's yours. The only problem with that is at the end of the day, your conscious eats at you like it's got some sort of hungry man munchies...that's if you have a conscious."

They walked the yard for the remaining few hours speaking about different events pertaining to them and the penitentiary circumstances.

Fuzzy and Freedom were becoming better acquainted

as the hours spun around the clock. Each one of them taking something from the other. Freedom needed these moments the most, for he was a *New Jack* in the concrete and steel jungle.

After recreation was over, Freedom went to the dayroom. He wanted to watch TV, but he found that hard to do. His mind was in the stratosphere somewhere contemplating and figuring. He was consumed with his thoughts, when a young guy came up to him and asked him was he watching the television. Freedom didn't answer him. It wasn't that he was ignoring dude like his mind was really surfing the wavelengths swishing and swashing around in his head. The young guy turned away and proceeded doing him. Freedom sat there for a while.

He got up and went to the phone. Maybe calling home would ease his mind and give him some resolve. His brother always had something worthwhile to discuss with him when they talked. This morning though, his mom picked up the call. He really didn't wanna talk to her right now. He finitely loves Mom' dukes, but he didn't feel like hearing a lecture on the good 'ole Lord Jesus Christ. She had plenty of high-flying names and attributes for this spiritual being nobody in the world could see in plain view. Blind faith is what you needed to get close to her God.

"Hi son. How're you?" She asked gaiety all in her voice. That was the *'Good Lord woke her up this morning'* energy.

Semaj sighed then retorted, "I'm good. Why you not at work this morning?"

"Well," she began. "Lemme see. I'm grown, took the day off, and been divorced from your dad for a few years now." Her mouth was slick and greasy as axel oil when she wanted to get you together. But that was his mom, who he loved more than life itself. Which really troubled him at times. He had ten years to do, and God forbid something happen to her along this bid.

They talked for a few minutes, which did help change the course of his spinning membrane. Then a C/O came into the pod and yelled that it was count time. And count time was a serious procedure here at Spring Valley. This is something he learned upon arriving on the compound. Remembering the confrontation, he had with that small fry ass pulling officer made him hurry up and reluctantly finish his phone call.

"I really gotta go to Ma. It's count time...I love you."

"Okay son. I love you, too and I'm praying for your early release."

Just as he was hanging up, C/O Miles pranced through the door yelling for the pod to get to their cells it was count

the ASUNDER *Story*... PART ONE: ENTER THE FIRE

time. Him and Freedom locked eyes. He almost fed into whatever this little punk wanted. Suddenly, his mother's voice resonated in his head which caused Freedom to shake his head and smirk at the C/O.

Ah man. That was Officer Mile's fuel and he cranked it up!

"You see something funny Mr. Carter?" He then inched closer to Freedom like he was pulling up on his prey. "Do I look and sound funny to you?"

It took everything in Freedom's right mind not to feed gas to the fire. He walked past C/O Miles almost brushing him. Freedom was twice his weak ass size but if he touched him in any way, form, or fashion he would be French toast. He was pretty sure this little squat could metamorphose into four or five mean crackers and whip his ass because there was no meaner and tougher gang than the D.O.C. Officers, fucking you up for putting your hands on one of theirs.

"That's right boy. Keep it moving!" C/O Miles barked with his chest huffed up.

Freedom's mind was blown away at the nonchalant way this officer used racial epithets like they were everyday common and casual language.

As he reached his cell and walked in, the door almost

caught his backside...again. Freedom didn't even turn around. GS peeped the ongoing quarrel between them then quickly diverted his attention back to the TV. Freedom missed his glance and look of frustration on GS's face.

GS was reading one of his magazines called, *Black Politics*. Freedom thought that those were the only type of magazines he possessed. He asked him did he have a Sports Illustrated magazine and to Freedom's surprise...he pulled out two crates of magazines from under his bunk. One crate had nothing but business and political magazines. The other crate had porn and other various magazines like *Vibe, Black Man, DuPont Registry, Essence, old issues of Double XL*, and even *Jet*. Some of the magazines dated back to 1998.

Freedom guessed that must've been when GS fell from dope boy status on the outside. Hell, Freedom was barely twelve years old then. He picked up a Vibe magazine from '98. GS told him he was twenty-one years old at the time and was just getting adjusted to the penitentiary life. While Freedom was reading the magazine, C/O Golden and C/O Miles were conducting count. She looked in and waved. GS peeped how she looked at Freedom with lust filled eyes. He quickly made a mental note of this transaction. Freedom knew that he only received the job he told her to oblige him with for the phone

***the* ASUNDER *Story*... PART ONE: ENTER THE FIRE**

call he made for him.

Later, he'd pull up on her and let her know she better get her shit together and if she was doing something behind his back, she better not let him find out about it. It wouldn't be pretty for them if he did. He thought to himself that she's his bitch and if she thought she was gonna play him, she better tighten up those loose screws in her head. Besides, the only way he would let somebody like Freedom hit it was if he was dreaming and he couldn't stop him then.

Count finally cleared and GS left immediately when the doors popped (unlocked). Freedom was still reading the *Vibe* magazine. GS came back into the cell with some work in a raggedy ass sandwich bag. He dropped it on Freedom's bunk like 'nigga take this!' Freedom looked kind of puzzled and angry at the same time. He picked up the sack disregarding whatever the content was and put it on GS's TV. Freedom said harshly that he was straight. GS just placed the sack back inside his pockets, shrugged his shoulders, and left back out of the cell. When he was gone, Freedom thought to himself that GS had to have notice the change in him. It was strange that he was trying to offer him anything. Maybe GS's psyche was at work again and could feel something was up with both Ms. Golden and his Bunkie. Who gives two fucks though because

the ASUNDER Story... PART ONE: ENTER THE FIRE

he wasn't any nigga's charity case? This nigga didn't give him anything, neither did he thank him for the task he'd already done for him. Suddenly, he wanna offer him some shit? Yeah right!? Then he got the nerve to give him leftovers, judging from the looks of the dirty sandwich bag.

"I don't know what this nigga takes me for?" he expressed to himself while looking at the walls.

He figured he was a step ahead of GS. He didn't know for how long he'd have the advantage. GS was guillotine sharp. Wait a minute, wait a minute, wait a minute. GS was more than head dismantling sharp. He was a goddamn mind reading bitch! He must remain solid and figure out how to stay in control though.

Ms. Golden gave him a portentous belief about the forces that she and he faced. GS was the X, Y, and Z factor seemingly in those forces. She also told him that if he could be a better man than GS, she would ride with him 'til the wheels and rubber burnt the car up.

Now that's a real rider, he thought. And somewhere in his head, he knew GS wasn't letting that whip drive off in the sunset, not without him not in it. Freedom knew for certain he wasn't dealing with a weak link; GS was older and with age came mad wisdom and he was endowed with plenty of

the ASUNDER Story...PART ONE: ENTER THE FIRE

wisdom. Freedom was young, inquiring, as well as wise; however, GS. possessed something that he himself was lacking. He was just going to play him close.

This was his third week on Spring Valley, and he'd almost done the unbelievable with an Officer and by now he was for sure he was winning her over. He was something to be reckoned with. He was self-made.

All the bumps, bruises, and scars he survived from is what made him official. He grew up from his trials and tribulations. That's why he was the man wherever and however.

His Pop's never saw any good in him. So, Semaj grew up bitter with his own ideations in life. He was tough like train nails. And the road to achievement never crossed or harkened on his doorstep. He grew up in the streets, and the family always moved around. They moved mostly up and down the East Coast except for once when his parents separated longer than usual. His mom took him and his sister, and her pregnancy to a small town in Kentucky called Fulton City.

In the small town of Fulton, he was too big of a presence. And that aura of cockiness lead to his earlier run-ins with the law and many of his peers. He didn't bow down nor

the ASUNDER Story...PART ONE: ENTER THE FIRE

submit. And sometimes you just had to turn the other cheek and that could probably save the other side of your ass. That's what his Momma would always tell him when he was flat out fuck it mode. Sometimes she'd tell him he was digging himself an early grave.

"No, I'm not Momma!" He'd shoot back. Then he'd go right out and get himself in the dirtiest ruts you could possibly uproot without a shovel. She loved him immensely, but she appreciated the times when he was off in a juvey institute or a county jail. She felt he was safe from his own destructive self.

He was a man now. A thinking man was what he considered himself to be. His potential to self-destruct was no longer who he was. And he was gonna be ready when it was time for exit stage left. He'd properly groom himself, and in turn his self-worth would one day be appreciated by his family, mainly his younger brother.

He felt that his brother was going to be the successor out of the family. Daniel strived daily to success. He also made a promise to Semaj that he'd make it in life and take his older brother with him on the road to success. So far, the road seemed clear. Daniel was in school in Brooklyn, New York. He was majoring in Fashion Arts and Business. He's already accomplished all his short-term goals. Now with only two

the ASUNDER Story... PART ONE: ENTER THE FIRE

years left before obtaining his bachelor's, and with a prominent clothing idea in the making, he was making things happen. Semaj was determined to help him get
the bread up that he needed to get his show on the road from rags to riches. Undoubtedly their family would soon be fortunate the way in which he always dreamed. After thinking heavily on things, he clapped his hands together and rubbed them like washing all his problems away. He had a plan, and it was time to put that plan into motion.

A crowd of inmates were gathered in one area. Freedom wasn't the nosey type; however, the crowd had an alluring feel to it. And whatever was going on might be in his best interest. He went to check things out. When he got there, some of the inmates started making an opening for him as if he was Phantom of the Opera. He noticed the man on the ground immediately. It was 'Lil Mike leaking blood from his stomach like a mini spigot. Freedom was getting ready to help him up, but someone grabbed his arm. It was one of the Bloods he saw with Max. He shook his head as if to tell Freedom not to bother the man on the ground. He didn't understand why he shouldn't help 'Lil Mike, but he left the situation be. The crowd began dispersing. The Blood who grabbed his arm asked him if he had some form of entertainment for a day or so because they would be on lockdown for at least two days.

The tower alarm sounded off with a blaring shriek. Freedom looked around anxiously and saw heavily shielded black uniforms marching in unison to the yard. As they were entering through the fence, everybody began lying down where they stood placing their hands behind their heads. Freedom instinctively followed suit. The men in black moved fast and quiet apprehending 'Lil Mike up from the ground along with the medical staff. They rolled him onto the stretcher and wheeled him away. Freedom looked up in time to see him holding what appeared to be his guts. He turned his head away from the grotesque scene.

After the nurses evaluated the premises, the lead man blew his whistle and started yelling for everyone to get up and file in single lines. They moved precautious, Freedom hadn't witnessed anything like this and seeing this for the first time prompted him to move accordingly just like everyone else. He felt like one wrong move would have him dispatched immediately.

When everyone entered the building, they were put on lockdown. GS was already in the room watching CNN News.

the **ASUNDER** *Story*...**PART ONE: ENTER THE FIRE**

He asked him if he seen 'Lil Mike fucked up in the game. He lied and told him that he didn't see him. He wondered how GS knew what the fuck happened when he was already in the cell. Reading right through his mind, GS made a comment that seemed more rancorous than informing.

"Young buck, niggas here don't play when it comes to their shit. Listen, there are three things you don't fuck with in the pen...one, a man's bitch as in his boy or C/O (he put emphasis on C/O) ...two, his money and last...a man's religion. Stay outta all that shit, and you'll remain alive."

He told Freedom that 'Lil Mike was seen coming out of an old timer's cell with his peoples. Somebody knew the old head and told him. 'Lil Mike was on the rec yard shooting craps. He never saw it coming. The old head walked up to the dice game, and as soon as 'Lil Mike stood up to leave, the old gangsta hit 'em up.

"'Lil Mike couldn't even fight back 'cause he was too busy holding his guts and lunch," GS retorted snickering at his own words.

Freedom listened to him somewhat dismayed. He wondered if what GS was telling him is what really happened or maybe he had 'Lil Mike set up, but for what and why? He thought about everything GS expressed, especially the part

the ASUNDER *Story*...PART ONE: ENTER THE FIRE

when he mentioned something about remaining alive.

Freedom changed the topic and asked GS how he could get some work in through the visit. GS gave him the rundown. He really didn't give two shits about what GS was talking about. Freedom was beginning to realize that the man that occupied the 6'x8' with him was a mere reflection of Beelzebub.

Suddenly, Freedom didn't wanna use any of his shit. He didn't even wanna be around him. He had to deal with that part though. They talked a while longer before Freedom admitted he was tired. He wasn't tired at all. He was only weary and worried a bit. He laid down, turned and faced the wall and began thinking things out. GS might be too much for him. He was powerful. Not only did he have plenty of money, but he also demanded respect, even if he subtly made you respect him. He was an enigma almost any way more than a problem. And he seemed to be Lord over this arena.

They say the greatest trick the devil ever played was convincing the world that he didn't exist. Freedom begged to differ. The devil wanted the world to know of his existence. Oh yeah, he did. The part we mostly fail to realize is which form he exists in. He was a montage of deception and trickery. And GS was one of his faithful stewards.

the ASUNDER *Story*...PART ONE: ENTER THE FIRE

Finally dozing off to sleep, Freedom had a dream that GS was holding a blood-ridden toddler. He was laughing at Freedom. Mockery and hate encompassed his face. He held the child out to him encouraging Freedom to get the child. It seemed like some sticky tentacles held him at bay. This was a nightmare. Finally able to move and as he got closer to GS, his laughter became amplified almost to a thunderous roar. He finally reached what was once GS and now had turned into a horrid looking mouth, with incisors like shark teeth. Somehow this child that GS was holding was now clung to one of the incision's crying. As Freedom reached out to save the youth, the tooth the toddler was hanging onto broke off and fell into some endless abyss. He fell into the black hole trying to save the child.

He woke up drenched in sweat. The room was almost pitch black except for the light coming from the catwalk or the tier. Freedom looked over at GS who appeared to be sound asleep. His body lain upward arms slightly skewed off his chest as if he was in a casket. And the silhouette distorting his face made it seem like he had a sinister smirk on it. Freedom lied back down but couldn't get back to sleep. He couldn't help but to wonder who and what GS really was.

the ASUNDER Story... PART ONE: ENTER THE FIRE

Chapter 3

the ASUNDER *Story*...PART ONE: ENTER THE FIRE

Scratch My Book and I'll Scratch Yours

The temporary lockdown lasted a day. Freedom got to learn more about GS and vice versa. He had a better interpretation as to what made GS tick. His life was about as soft as the concrete that twenty-three hundred inmates walked and ran every day. The history he gave Freedom was repeating itself, only in live action.

Godfrey was six and a half years when his older sister Amera and his mom were sexually assaulted by some gang members belonging to the gang called the West Side Vipers (Romelio's rivals). As they were leaving one of the gang members came back in and was shot and killed by a young Godfrey. Then he waited for the rest of them to come back, which they never did. At that moment he didn't care whether he lived or died. After making his first kill, he got on the phone and called his dad and told him what transpired at their home.

For the next few weeks, several Viper gang members were brutally slain. Romelio took his son along the killing spree and at times would let Godfrey participate in cold murders. Soon enough Godfrey acquired a ravenous taste for blood, emulating his dad almost like a book. Romelio Kayne Sevens was known for drug trafficking and his sanguinary hitman squad. Every week a body was found in dumpsters or plain sight in the streets...the streets of Watts California feared and respected his reign and power. All who imposed him, or his son were either killed or made to believe that if they crossed them, they would pay with their lives or their families' lives.

Romelio suffered from not having a father figure, probably bringing about his misguided aggression. They lived in the village of Fullarton Trinidad. His mother Geneva worked hard to maintain what they had, which was a small shack. The two main means of livelihood in the area were fishing and coconuts. Although she constantly worked and made a living for them, it was never enough. She yearned to be in the U.S. of A and with every effort to get there, one day she'd make it.

Geneva and her son left Trinidad one hot summer night on a cargo ship that got them to the shores of California. The ship was dropping off crab barrels, fish crates, illegal immigrants, poppy plants, and sugar cane. The trip was exhausting, but they made it safely to California.

Their new life in California was supposed to be promising, prominent and different, but it really wasn't too

the ASUNDER *Story*... PART ONE: ENTER THE FIRE

much better than the Island. Her son was going through a metamorphosis she couldn't understand. The weather couldn't be the determining factor in his behavior. The sun scorched on them in Cali as it did in Trinidad. It might've been the sporadic continent change. She still hoped that Watts would've offered so much more.

Geneva and Romelio worked long hard days and nights in some of the most retched motels in Watts. She had just enough money by the weekend to pay off where they stayed. At times she'd take her son to food markets and use him for a decoy as she shoplifted for food. One time she was caught stealing in a local family business. She and her son were taken to the manager's office. Geneva begged the manager not to call the police because they would know that they were illegal immigrants. And worse they'd probably take her only son. The store owner called two of his sons into the office to discuss how the woman should pay for her larcenous crime.

They decided to make her commit sexual acts and made her seven-year-old son watch. Romelio was forced to watch for brutal hours of lecherous dogs use and abuse his mom. She would eventually pass out from the physical trauma. Romelio sat in the chair too petrified and angry to cry. When they were

the ASUNDER *Story*... PART ONE: ENTER THE FIRE

done with her, she and her son were driven to an abandoned building and left there. One of the men pulled out a gun and pointed it at Romelio and gestured to shoot him. This was mockery and disregard for human life. Finally, they drove away leaving sounds of vile laughter lingering through his ears. He crawled up beside his mother and cried himself to sleep on her slow but steady heavy breasts, breathing. Before falling asleep, he made his first promise. He promised himself that when he was old enough, he was gonna kill the man and his sons and whoever else claiming to be family with those sadistic animals.

Romelio was a small-time hustler working for the man who raped his mother. At the time of Geneva's assault, he was barely seven years old. So, when he went to work for the Montero family at the ripen age of fourteen, they never remembered him. He endured through every irrational thought in order to sustain his composure and job as one of the Montero's runners.

On a hot July 7th day, Romelio and a few of his comrades brutally slayed and chopped off the heads, hands, and penises of two Montero family members, one of the sons and a cousin. Their demise made heavy publicity and the Montero family was infuriated. Especially Razón, who was the sole proprietor of the family. With the power he had established in Watts, he knew no one who would have the audacity to oppose him or his peoples. He was gonna find the culprit and when he did, he was gonna paint the city in graffiti with their blood. What he failed to realize was that his enemy was a teenage boy, who had a promise to fulfill. Romelio's job wasn't done.

Razón Montero was the father of the family and the man who made his mom commit ungodly shit. Razón was the fuel to his fire and rampage. A year later, Romelio would kill again. Razón was barely seen. He was the man supplying a large percentage of Watts heroine. Seeing him was tough as train nails. Then he met Anita Montero. It would be her who would unknowingly help Romelio kill her father.

The Watts Academy School of Arts ring dance was on the special night of July 7, 1969. He escorted beautiful Anita to the dance. She took him to meet her father. Razón was much older then. Either he was going through the first stages of dementia, or Romelio wasn't that important to remember. That was fine by him because he'd remember him when the time was right.

Razón was protected like a Brinks armored truck: two gatemen, two doormen, and interrogating butler and video cameras. When Romelio seen this, he fell into a stint of despair. He was determined though even if it cost him his life.

Anita and he were given first class treatment to the dance. When they entered the school, he immediately went to spike the punch. He added some 80-proof homemade corn liquor to it. It was jet fuel and by the end of the night, Anita was inebriated.

The chauffer was vexed. Razón was gonna have a field day. Anita was his only daughter, and she had been sheltered. This was her first night out without her father in company. Which would've never even been considered under any other circumstances. She was out with this young punk and a chauffeur whose duty was to make sure nothing happened to her. The young boy didn't seem to be drunk or tipsy. In fact, he was well composed. He was responsible for this and when he reached Razón's estate, he was gonna put the blame on him.

"We'll see how composed you are in the presence of a real man," the chauffer whispered to no one, looking at the young guy in the rearview mirror.

When the limousine pulled up to the gates of the estate, Romelio became nervous. He wasn't scared of dying at all. He was prepared to meet his maker. More or less, he was worried that things wouldn't go as planned.

the ASUNDER *Story*... PART ONE: ENTER THE FIRE

After getting in the home, Romelio realized that one of the doormen had been relieved of his duties. That left only five men to kill, Razón included. He hoped he only had to kill who he came here for. Killing this many men by yourself might be hard as hell.

Anita was carried away to her bedroom. And after what seemed like forever waiting to be seen, he was finally ushered upstairs to Razón's office room. He talked down to him for the incident. After he finished with his rant and rave getting his point across, he told the butler to take Romelio home. And he is to never be seen or heard of being with his daughter again.

Before leaving, Romelio asked the butler if he could use the bathroom. The butler was agitated. He grabbed his arm and abruptly pulled him to the bathroom. Once he got in the bathroom, he pulled out his .25 caliber and screwed on the muffle assembly. Then he opened the door and asked the butler to come check why the toilet wouldn't flush. The butler signed heavily and moved him out of the way. After flushing the toilet, he turned around to say something, a bullet hit him right between the eyes dropping him instantly. He cut off the bathroom light and closed the door. He went to face Razón for the last time.

the ASUNDER *Story*... PART ONE: ENTER THE FIRE

As he opened the door, Razon was talking on the phone, his back was turned to him. He approached him quietly. He listened to Razon as he talked about a drug shipment. He had no heart. He probably never checked on his daughter. She could be getting raped by one of his trusted men, just as his mother was and this pathetic excuse of a man is on the phone talking about a drug shipment. As he hung up the phone, he spun around in his chair and almost choked on his tongue. He reached for his intruder button.

"Don't even think about it. You fat fuck!" Romelio said angrily with his gun drawn out.

"You can have anything you want...just don't—"

"Shut the fuck up!" Razon exclaimed roughly cutting him off. "Now listen to what I gotta say."

Razon did as he was told. Romelio took him back to the day when him and his two sons raped his mom and made him watch. The past was the past. Razon stressed that he was sorry and that he would give him anything he asked for.

"Fuck off!" Romelio almost shouted. Then he shot him in both knees. He fell out of his chair, while squealing like some wild pig that knows it's about to be butchered.

"You yell or get loud again, I'll kill you."

"Okay, okay," Razon hissed holding both his knees.

the ASUNDER *Story*...PART ONE: ENTER THE FIRE

Romelio walked over to the man and stood over top of him, gun aimed in his face.

"Tell me why I shouldn't smoke 'yo ass!?"

Razon didn't have anything to say. He just stared into the blank black eyes of a murderer.

Romelio shot him again, this time in the head that he used to ejaculate on his mom's face. Razon did everything in his power not to scream. Somewhere in his mind he believed that Romelio would just torture him then leave, happy to have revenged his mother. He shot him a coupla more times in areas that would definitely render his chances for doing anything. He begged for the torture to stop. He walked over to the fireplace, grabbed the stoker, and heated it up. When Razon saw what he was doing, he knew then. He asked him if he could see his daughter. He ignored his request. When he pulled the stoker from the fire, it was read orange.

He walked over to the man who tried yelling but was brought to a quick halt. When the stoker went into his mouth. He couldn't even whimper then. Finally, he rolled Razon on his back and drove the hot piece of iron up his rectum. He let out a pungent odor. Romelio was enjoying every bit of the torture he was putting him through. The phone rang, he was caught off guard. It was time for him to get outta there. He stood over

Razon and put two shots in the back of his head, ending his life. Then he left through the room balcony, nothing on his mind but his mother.

GS claimed that Romelio and his young family moved to Delaware a year or so after his mother and sister were sexually assaulted. His dad tied up a few more loose strings before leaving California. He didn't wanna take a suitcase of West Coast life to the East Coast. A drug lord doesn't give up territory that easily though. Romelio was still heavily tied to California. It was his undying angel. Their lives changed as far as the land goes, but their lifestyle never altered. Wherever Romelio was, there was blood, murder, and drugs.

Eventually Romelio started his clothing business. Sevens attire gear to become the most popular urban wear of the nineties. His dad didn't really get to see his business become an empire. He was accidentally shot and killed by federal officers leaving the business to his son.

Which takes you to the present. GS really was an entrepreneur. He was a survivor as well. He showed Freedom some of the business credentials. All the paperwork seemed legitimate, but his intuition was strong. Every time it came

the ASUNDER Story...PART ONE: ENTER THE FIRE

time for him to learn an individual, he never misjudges them. His mother told him that God gave him the gift of discerning people. However, it was that one time he could be wrong. He was just gonna have to let the situation unravel. It seemed like GS was dealt the wrong hand, somewhat like he had been. Time will tell.

They hadn't seen Ms. Golden in two days, which was strange to them because she worked almost every day of the week. If she decided not to come to work on any basis it was Saturday and or Sunday. It was the middle of the week. She might just be taking time off. GS thought that he knew all her moves. Maybe he was losing her. To whom or what was questionable. But if he could put his finger on it, it would ease immediately just as fast as it started. He did all the thinking for her, no Freedom, not any of the other inmates, or the officers in that case. When she first came to Spring Valley, she was an ordinary green C/O.

The very first day, Angelón Christian Golden walked onto the compound she was naturally scared. In her training seminar she was told some lies and some truths. The only thing that frightened her the most was when the Warden told the women that they could be raped, raped *and* stabbed, or raped *and* killed. He also told them never to trust the inmates.

the ASUNDER *Story...* PART ONE: ENTER THE FIRE

Especially the inmates of color for their line of deceit extended beyond their control. Angelón wanted to forget she even came to the training course and run. She couldn't possible do that though and go back to her homeland.

She was born and raised in Kennesaw, Georgia.
Her mother died a few hours after her coming into the world. She wanted a child so bad. Her pregnancy was complicated. Angelón was Sherri Goldens only child given to her from God's grace. She supposedly couldn't conceive. Doctors mentioned that if she were to have a baby, a C-Section would be the best option for her and the newborn. And after weighing her options, she decided to have a baby one day. Finally, Sherri's prayers were answered, and she became pregnant, and she rejoiced in the Lord.

Her husband Derick was not enthused about her being pregnant either. He drank too much and when drinking didn't do enough for him, drugs would suffice. He felt that Sherri having a baby was gonna take away from his hard-earned money. And if that happened it would be less booze and less drugs.

He did his best trying to convince her to abort the baby that would eventually take her life. Such a determined woman his wife was-losing her first born wasn't an option, not even to some vacuum that sucked a fetus from the womb.

Sherri continued to work as a waitress. She worked hard, not only to take care of her conceived baby, but to leave Derick once her baby was born. Everyone at her job was happy for her. Sometimes they'd get upset with her because she would come to work bruised up from Derick and hadn't left him sooner.

Derick was always blowing a fuse. And when Sherri would try and talk to him about attending NA and AA meetings, he just would let it go though. Indulgence was his life and Sherri and their unborn was too much like right, killing the high lights.

So, on that wild night of extra drinking, this night would be remembered as overkill to him. He had gotten so smashed that he could vaguely remember beating his wife almost to a bloody pulp. Furthermore, bring on her delivering Angelón prematurely.

He was in handcuffs that night Angelón Christian Golden was born. Bless her soul, Sherri passed away a few hours later. It was a beautiful and sad night. Although the magnitude of the night belonged to the child, the death of Sherri and the lock up of Derick invented the malfunction of

the ASUNDER Story... PART ONE: ENTER THE FIRE

the night's splendor. The doctors did all they could to manage saving Sherri, but after examining the X-rays she suffered from head trauma, a couple of broken ribs, and a fractured shoulder. With all that abuse and the early labor, brung on Sherri's untimely demise.

After his daughter was born, Derick was carried away to the county jail and Angelón was soon after placed in foster care. She never had the chance to be raised by her God-fearing mother.

Derick did fifteen months in the county jail for spousal abuse. Five years was placed over his head, and he was released on unsupervised probation. Upon his release, he was to attend court ordered NA and AA meetings for a year, three days a month. Then the judge would resummon him to court to attain custody of his only child.

Derick was attentive and punctual to each meeting sharing his mishaps in life, from the use of drugs and alcohol. Now with his personal relationship with the Lord Jesus Christ, he was getting his life back on track.

A year later, he was given full custody of his daughter. She was two years old then. And at first things were going great for the both of them. Then he had gotten in a serious accident on his roofing job. He was receiving workers compensation. It was just enough to pay rent, somewhat take care of his daughter, and buy booze. That's the trigger for an old gun inflicting his old wounds.

Angelón was five years old the day her dad sexually molested her. He told her that he had to keep her clean and that touching her was a part of the procedure. He told her that if she ever mentioned anything to anybody, he would spank her so hard that her mother would come back from the dead only to get in the way if she tried to stop him.

Angelón was abused and molested all the way up to the age of thirteen. Growing sick of her dad's nasty ass, she upped and ran away from home. She became missing in action for about two years. Angelón was found by a detective who found her stripping in a local strip club. The detective was at the strip bar on an investigation, which stemmed from an inside source claiming that the club was employing underage girls. The detective had seen her face in the newspaper. The night he noticed her; he intuitively knew who she was. She was incredibly beautiful, vivacious, and full of life. He took her home that night.

Once they got to his home, he told her to wait in the living room while he went to freshen up. He went to his bedroom and called a squad car to come pick her up. When they took her into custody, she fought and cursed them to high heaven. She was taken to the county jail. They called her father who wasn't available at the time; however, a message was left for him to get in contact with them as soon as possible. When her dad didn't call the sheriff office back in 48 hours, a foster home was the next option.

After two months of malicious and mean comments along with petty squabbles with the older boys and girls, she decided to go home and face the ugly music.

Angelón was released to her father a few days later. Derick told her that he'd changed and that he was a born-again Christian who had been washed by the blood of the lamb. And for a while, things seem to have gotten better. The two of them attended church. They went out as a family recovering from tough times and most importantly Derick hadn't had a drink of alcohol since she's been back home. It could be a holy reunion after all.

He decided to have some champagne one night and drink to his new relationship with his daughter and God. And that's when old imps woke up the deep lecherous monster in his mind and body. He snuck into her room while she was asleep. Then he raped her with brute forces that had come from the pits of a dirty stinking place in hell. He beat her telling her she was the reason he didn't have a wife anymore. And she was the devil's worker, who caused him to sin.

She fought and pleaded with him to stop, but he overpowered her with ease. When he finished, he left a battered and bruised Angelón locked up in her room. Then he boarded up the door to her room, as well as the outside windows to her room and made her a prisoner in her own home. If she needed to use the bathroom, she was afforded a potty. He fed her good and the nights he came in and her food wasn't eaten, he'd force feed her, reassuring her that he didn't want a skinny little helpless heifer. Days when he was gone, she would scream to the top of her lungs hoping that someone would hear her. But that was hopeless because every home in the neighborhood was at least a half a mile away.

She lived as a prisoner in her bedroom for fourteen months until one night when her dad came to sex her, she had miraculously got a nail out of one of the boards on the window. Derick had straddled over top of her for the last time with his stinking wine breath. He began licking and playing with her nipples, at the same time forcing his rough textured fingers inside her vagina, hurting her on more. She stabbed him in the ear sending him into a frenzy of anger and pain. Now was the time.

the ASUNDER Story... PART ONE: ENTER THE FIRE

The door wasn't locked. She bolted out of the room. He tried to grab her but the injury to his ear was viciously painful and hindered him momentarily from doing so. She ran into the living room and tried dialing 911. She was shaking uncontrollably and dialing three easy numbers was impossible. Her father was on his way yelling for her as he came in pursuit. She dropped the phone down and ran out of the front door bare chested, moving with collected speed she never imagined having. She was free. She ran until the flat of her feet became bloody and bruised. She slowed down to walk in the quiet town of Kennesaw, she laughed and cried, but happy to never be seen by her father again.

After being took on a mock shakedown. She seen him. GS was the man that would change her whole life.
Her and GS would be seen conversating, but it was casual. She found comfort in him.

Once an inmate tried to force himself on her. She got away from him; however, she didn't report the incident for fear of losing her job. A few weeks later, she would explain to GS that the man was found stabbed to death in one of the vocational class bathrooms. She asked him if he did it. He didn't even know the man, he claimed. Angelón didn't condone in murdering a man. She had found God the day she escaped her father. And she believed that God would take vengeance on all her transgressors.

After GS explained to her that he knew nothing of the man's death. She believed him somewhat. She told him that God would reveal all things done by man in due time. GS never cared about God. This Almighty spook allowed his mother and sister to be raped, his grandmother was raped before, and God never protected them. To him God was a ghost that only existed in people's head who allowed themselves to toy with his eminence. GS was very cold hearted. However, Ms. Golden found comfort in him. Everyone on the grounds of Spring Valley never tried anything with her. For they all learned that death would be waiting for them with open arms. Ms. Golden herself had a healthy fear of GS. But she was comfortable with him and has been by his side and only his side since.

The next day, CO Golden came to work in high spirits. GS was glad she was back in his presence. She told GS that she needed some days off to make some self-improvements. GS laughed and asked her what for? She was good enough for him and that was all she needed to understand. She expressed to him that she needed to make changes. She didn't want to spend the rest of her life as a C/O. She wanted a child. Someone to keep her company at night away from him. GS wasn't feeling this new Angelón or her abrupt changes.

"What's up with you Angelón?" He asked her, stressing her name, which he didn't use often because of the environment.

"Nothing really important baby. I just don't wanna live this way anymore. I wanna quit and get married." She knew that GS didn't wanna talk about marrying her because he didn't wanna get married. He felt that being married was such a burden. And she wouldn't get to see him until the weekends, of course at another institution. Then he would promise her that he was gonna eventually make parole or get a new trial which would set him free, and they could be together as they so pleased. Ms. Golden was finding life in someone new. It wasn't so much about their rendezvous, which took her by storm. It was the look in Freedom's eyes when she talked to him. He had the natural efficacy that made not just her, but anyone believe he was going places. Freedom was everything GS wasn't. He was kindhearted, he cares about her feelings first and foremost. He also hadn't been with any other woman on Spring Valley correctional center since he'd gotten there, and he listed to her without shooting down her thoughts.

the ASUNDER Story... PART ONE: ENTER THE FIRE

GS knew something else was going on with her. He really didn't give a shit if she quit or not, because where else would she go without his support?

He had brought her a car, a small home in Dover, Delaware, as well as proposed to her. Although that wasn't serious. Fact of the matter was GS made her who she is now. Which was more than she'd ever been.

"If you were glass and I dropped you, would you be unbreakable?" GS asked her.

The question caught her off guard. When she didn't respond GS continued.

"My thought exactly...you're nothing without us my little Angel." He said, then laughed at her walking away leaving her to think about all she had to lose without him.

Fuzzy and Freedom were bonding closer day by day. Fuzzy looked at Freedom like the son he could never have. Freedom had dreams and aspirations. He was going places without hurting the people he needed to get there. Although Fuzzy had groomed GS into a fine convict, GS wanted blood with every situation. Fuzzy latched on to GS the moment he came to Spring Valley Correctional Center. GS was mentally sophisticated and determined to be more than his father; or at least amount up to him.

the ASUNDER *Story*...PART ONE: ENTER THE FIRE

Fuzzy knew about Romelio by reading the papers but he suffered greatly from deprivation of heart and spirit. He was believed to have killed with grace. And he eluded all of the good 'ole boys with an ease. Even though Fuzzy didn't meet GS's father, GS emulated him in ways that instilled a healthy fear in him. The fear wasn't a scary kind; more or less at times a regretful tithe with him that he feared he would one day have to sever.

He was never going home, but God made exceptions for the humble and meek. And if God was gonna help him ever come home, he'd have to alleviate some of those rough edges that bound him to prison and the politics of it. Fuzzy was tryna live as a born-again saint, and many nights he'd pray to God to heal him of his wicked ways, but with GS attached to his right hand, being saved and sanctified almost didn't matter. God knew his heart though. And he was a new man. His yes-ter-years did nothing in justifying who he was today.

Fuzzy was born in Brooklyn, New York and raised in Harlem. He was born to Marcus and Sandra Reynolds. Michael Reynolds, now Fuzzy was mentally and physically abused by his dad and scorned constantly by his mom.

Michael grew up neglected by his parents and many of his peers, unless it was discipline time, or he was fighting.

the ASUNDER Story...PART ONE: ENTER THE FIRE

Michael was born with eleven fingers and eleven toes. Sandra naturally wanted these limbs removed, but they were numb, and after thorough information from the doctors. The deformity wasn't an issue in fact it might be helpful. It definitely made him different.

Both of his parents loved and hated him. They loved him because he was their son and hated him because of his deformities and what he might've done to a brother or sister Sandra was supposed to have had. In her womb during pregnancy, she was told she would be expecting twins. She was overwhelmed with joy. Until after an ultrasound revealed that one of the twins had been depleted, either from the lack of food being received by one of the twins or one of the twins were consumed by the other. Suddenly Sandra wanted an abortion. She felt that an evil spawn was in her womb.

But after heavy convincing from her husband, he made her believe that the seed left in her couldn't have possibly done what the doctors assumed, because everybody was born innocent. Michael came a month after the ninth month. After she held her newborn child she looked into his eyes. They were barely open, but what she seen in her newborn's eyes were enough to make her almost drop him. Marcus grabbed him.

"What's wrong with you Sandra!" he asked her uneasily. She'd been crying. The way she was sobbing, one would be forced to believe that the child died during delivery. Marcus held his newborn son high smiling. Then he noticed his son's deformity. He wasn't as much as bothered by that; it was what the doc's had said that could've happened during Sandra's pregnancy that bothered him. Maybe this was a child of the evil one. Marcus gave his son to doctors for Michael to receive his first initial whipping to open his lungs to breath better. The doctor obliged. Michael began crying, but not a tear shed. His cry was more like an angry yell.

They returned home a couple of days later. A lot of the family was there waiting to see the bundle of joy. When Sandra and Marcus walked in with Michael their home was filled with joyous yelling and party horns Everyone seem to be in glee— everybody accept the lifers of the party. The noise simmered down.

"What's wrong baby?" Sandra mentioned depressingly enough and gave the baby to her husband.

"Well let me hold my grandbaby," Evelyn gestured.

Marcus passed the child to his mother-in-law. She removed the veil from over her grandbaby's face. She didn't say a word. That caused everyone to move closer to Evelyn and

the ASUNDER *Story*...PART ONE: ENTER THE FIRE

the baby. Some people were saying things that normally would make a proud dad tell everyone to get the hell out of his house. But that they were commenting on was right.

"Boy you got 'yo daddy's features, but these eyes are black and mean as they come," Evelyn said lightly. She still was smiling. Then she motioned for everyone to join hands so they can pray.

After praying, some of the family left as if they were disappointed. Those that stayed around were eating and talking amongst themselves. Evelyn got up and went to her daughter. Marcus followed her. After they entered the room, she gave the baby to Marcus. He closed the door and went and sat on the bed next to his mother-in-law and wife, who seemed to be asleep. Evelyn started rubbing Sandra's head. She opened her eyes looked at her mom and began to whine.

"Shhh girl. You'll wake the baby," Evelyn said quietly.

"Momma, what have we...what have I done?" Sandra asked through soft sobs.

"Listen baby, this ain't your fault. Lemme tell you a story... your father, my deceased husband was a man of God when it was convenient. See, when you were just three years old, he killed himself."

Sandra began to interrupt with protest as Evelyn

the ASUNDER *Story*... PART ONE: ENTER THE FIRE

continued.

"I know. I know. I told you he had a stroke. See baby, you were the world to your daddy. You two were inseparable. But the truth always has to come to the light. Your dad fell in love with another woman. She was a voodoo witch. Your father had been coming from church one cold night and seen the woman being beaten by another man. Your daddy paused for a minute.

I guess he was assessing the situation. He finally rolled down the car window and told the man to stop beating the woman. The man looked at your dad and told him the fuck off...excuse my French. Anyhow, your father wasn't a man of violence. So, he rolled up the window and drove up the next block. He pulled over and got out and went to the closest payphone to call the police."

She continued. "As he was dialing 911, the scene was still in plain view. Out of nowhere the man beating the lady up dropped in cold blue. It wasn't the fact of him dropping, it was what he heard from the woman's assailant. Your dad told me that the man screamed with an agonizing pain so intense that some of the man's pain registered in him. By this time, your father had dropped the phone and got back into the car. He had been drinking that night after church. He would say he drank

the **ASUNDER** *Story...* **PART ONE: ENTER THE FIRE**

because Jesus drank wine. You know they say Jesus turned water into wine...you know that story."

Evelyn tried to make the couple smile a bit. They were intensely listening to her. When they didn't budge, she resumed.

"Anyhow, he figured he had too much to drink that night. The woman stood up from her disposition and looked at your father's car. He was looking at her in the rearview mirror. Then he said he heard the woman laughing. A laugh that was painfully sexy and wicked simultaneously. He claims he eventually put the pedal to the medal and peeled out of there." Evelyn waited for that part of the story to register.

Sandra spoke up. "Momma where is all this going?" Evelyn sighed before continuing.

"Well, this is the part that hurts me so much. You know some weeks later, that same woman came to church. He claimed she was very beautiful. Her magnetic attraction is what...it's what got him in her bed that day."

Evelyn bowed her head and let out a small whimper. Marcus put his arm around Evelyn in an attempt to console her. Sandra clicked her teeth not moved by her mother's burden.

"Momma, I wanna know the truth and what's really

going on with this mistake of a baby I done gave birth to?" Sandra exclaimed harshly.

Evelyn carried on.

"You know he came home that night a changed man. Not a good changed man. He started drinking more heavily and stopped going to church. He would've moved out had it not been for you. He just stopped loving me, Sandra. And after he found out about this woman's lifestyle and Voodoo practices, he panicked. I mean a Voodoo witch was way more than he had bargained for. But he couldn't stray away from her. He was trapped. And from the note he left me before he pulled a cowardice act of suicide, stated everything that happened between both he and her. He said that he would see her everywhere...Behind him, in his dreams, just every damn place she wasn't supposed to be.

Then one day he had you with him. He said he was holding you and a sharp pain went through his back. He almost dropped you. He was on his way upstairs to our apartment when he seen the bitch! He immediately put you down and approached her. They exchanged words and he almost put his hands on her quickly remembering what she was. He came back to get you and go inside. As y'all were going in the apartment, she blew you a kiss, the same way your daddy

the ASUNDER Story... PART ONE: ENTER THE FIRE

would do. Your dad would blow you kisses, and you would reach out and catch them and put them on your cheek. Automatically, you put her kiss on your cheek. You see the scar on your face wasn't an accident."

Sandra slowly rubbed her cheek where the scar was at. Everything her mother was saying sounded bizarre. Black magic wasn't processing in her psyche.

"You had started screaming as if you had gotten burnt. Your father rushed in the door; closed it, ran to the sink, and grabbed a cold rag. The rag didn't seem to be doing the job. So, he went to the icebox and grabbed some ice and massaged your cheek with it. Your screaming went almost down to a whimper. Then he put you to sleep. Afterwards he went into our bedroom and wrote the letter before taking his life. You never woke until the next day. When I came in the apartment and found you on the couch sleeping, I knew something was wrong, because your dad wouldn't never put you to sleep without tucking you in. I took you to your room tucked you in and prayed."

"Then I went in my room and found him sprawled out on the bed, gun and note beside him. I nearly lost it after reading that letter. Finally, I mustered up the courage to go to your room and confirm what your father had written. When I

the ASUNDER Story...PART ONE: ENTER THE FIRE

looked on your face and seen the fresh new mark, I got out the prayer oil and anointed you, your room, and damn near the entire apartment. You were cursed from your father's promiscuity." Evelyn finally finished. For a while the room was still and silent, as if life itself had crept out of existence. Sandra still rubbing the scar on her face finally spoke.

"Mom, why you ain't never tell me this until now god dammit!"

"Baby, I just didn't---," Evelyn was saying before her daughter cut her off.

"My damn life, my husband, and my fuckin' child is cursed because of your husband's bullshit! Momma, get outta my house!" Sandra spewed out angrily.

Marcus intervened. "Hold no now honey. Evelyn if this is true, why didn't you say something before. At least you coulda had the common decency to tell us when we told you were tryna have a baby."

"I'm sorry. I just didn't think anything of it. I was so happy y'all were having a baby. And then when you told me y'all were expecting twins, I was really overjoyed. Please forgive me baby."

Sandra was sobbing heavily. Evelyn put her arm around her daughter. She continued to cry on her mother's shoulder.

the ASUNDER *Story*...PART ONE: ENTER THE FIRE

The situation was what it was. The only thing that made sense now was to pray and hope that the Almighty would heal their household and issues.

Marcus was six years old when he committed his first murder knowingly. He had found a mut puppy in the laundry room in the basement of their apartment building. The whining mongrel irritated Michael for reasons he couldn't recollect. Once the puppy seen him, it ran to him. Michael picked up the puppy. It was licking him all over the face, fully not aware that its life was in jeopardy. He walked over to a laundry machine and put the animal in it. He then put some change in the slot and turned the dial to hot water. The hot water was scolding hot and pushed the button. The hot water came out steaming. The puppy was howling and trying to get out of the machine. Michael closed the machine's top. After the puppy ceased whining, he felt good.

Michael had hair on his face by the time he entered second grade. People in school and his parents started calling him Fuzzy bear. Michael hated that name and beefed with anyone who called him that. He tolerated his parents. So fighting was an everyday thing for him.

He came in from a basketball game one hot summer afternoon and wanted to hop right in the shower. His dad was in the bathroom showering and singing away like he was about to get a music deal. What a bitch. So Fuzzy banged on the door.

"Was'up Fuzzy?" Marcus asked him, opening the door exposing his naked self to his son.

"Man, I need to take a shower!" Michael demanded.

"Well Fuzzy, man when I'm done," his dad commented back and shut the door in his face. Michael went to his room and got on the phone. While he was talking to his homeboy, his mom picked up the phone.

"Oh, I'm sorry Fuzzy. Lemme know when you got off the phone," she expressed easily.

Michael was fed up to the brim. That night he shot his parents in their sleep. Afterwards he told himself there goes your *Fuzzy*. That night when the police came to pick him up he sat there on the edge of his parents' bed and when they asked him why he did it he just said Fuzzy.

Since then, Fuzzy had given his life to God Which was why he never cared too much for GS's vindictive nature. GS was his main man though. Whenever Fuzzy heard that GS had a man killed or he might've killed him, he'd ask God to forgive him for befriending a man such as GS.

When Fuzzy met Freedom, he automatically took a liking to him. Freedom eventually told him that he killed a man, but it was out of self-defense. It didn't make it right. However, he could tolerate Freedom's decision to do what he felt had to be done. And he wasn't a known killer as GS was. He was a young man who had a lot of potentials. And Fuzzy was gonna try to help the youngin live up to the prospects. Freedom wasn't naïve to his existence. He did need some assistance in understanding the dynamics of prison. And that's where he came in. Eager and willing to help Freedom along, put him under his wing, sorta speak.

GS seen and felt Fuzzy clinging to Freedom. He didn't take it personal though. He understood it the way it was, old school meets young world. And he's showing the kid the ropes, the same way Fuzzy gave him the game when he was young and inquiring.

Another thing that drew Fuzzy to Freedom was his listening ear. The young man listened to things. He asked questions and took heed to answers. Something GS stop doing a long while ago. He began to think that he would have to stray away from GS completely if he wanted to receive his blessing from God. But first he had to finish what he started. Things had to be completed in his life, GS's life, and most importantly Freedom's life.

The week had gone by fast bringing the weekend in

quickly. GS had talked to his sister, Amera Friday morning. She told him that she would come see him Saturday. He loved his older sister. She was a big part of his support group since he'd been incarcerated. He took care of his family since a young boy; when he should've been playing with video games, he was signing checks and cashing bank statements, bigger than what most people would make in a lifetime. He was the reason why his family were financially straight at the moment. He knew that if he didn't get back into court soon, all of his efforts to build up his legacy would soon dissipate. Time was of the essence. Seeing his sister this weekend meant one or two things...Either money was funny, or she had problems. A lot of their communication went through mail, and it had to be deciphered by Amera, reason of the Feds.

The Feds had been on to GS before and since he fell. They knew he would eventually get back to court with a new trial. But they would have strong enough evidence to re-indict him. This was Special Agent Mat Conner's belief. He had been onto the Sevens family since the early nineties. He had worked hard on bringing down Romelio and had come up short by a nose hair. He never could get him. Once Romelio passed away and gave the torch to his son, he swore by God that he would persecute his boy and bring an end to the Sevens.

the ASUNDER *Story*... PART ONE: ENTER THE FIRE

When GS had turned fourteen, he'd began living the life of crime such as his dad. The State of Delaware indicted him a week before his fifteen birthday and declared him innocent two months later. That frustrated Mat. He knew that if the state had done enough to convict him, he in turn would have been able to indict him with more charges dating back to when he was twelve years old. The breakthrough that he was striving to make happen seemed so close yet very distant.

All his years as an agent and bringing down any cartel, killer, a bank robber, and anyone else was not so arduous, but this family were too elusive. By the time GS had turned seventeen, he thought he had finally got him. Somehow GS wiggled his way out of their hands and was sentenced by the state. Mat still didn't have enough evidence to bring the reign of the family to a closure. In fact, the conviction of the DA was so fragile, he knew GS would soon be back on the streets. He had too much power and money. Blood money that would pay for his return back to the land of the free. His sworn duty to himself was to take down the Sevens empire. And by God he was going to or die trying.

GS's sister, Amera had told him she had some good news for him and when she came to deliver the good news Saturday, his bid was gonna change for the better. He was

the ASUNDER *Story*... PART ONE: ENTER THE FIRE

anxious for Saturday to get here. He didn't know what to expect. What could possibly be good news? Maybe his lawyer, Jonathan Braxwood had finally found the loophole in his case. But he had just talked to his lawyer that night before and attorney Braxwood had told him no good news yet.

"We'll just have to wait and see," GS mentioned to himself. It was after lockdown and Freedom went to rest early. GS was listening to his CD Player. Tomorrow's news would shed some light on a few things. When he talked to Amera, she seemed elated about whatever it was she had to talk to him about. He couldn't really sleep. He had so many things running through his mind.

"My time to shine is now...whatever Amera has to talk about, it's only gonna add to my power," GS was telling himself about things around him. Then out of nowhere, he looked over at Freedom who was sound asleep.

"You think I'mma let you out do me young gangsta? It'll never happen in this lifetime." He laughed at his own words. He turned off his JP5, then dozed off to sleep.

When Freedom had awoken Saturday morning, GS was gone. The TV was on. He decided to watch it. Fuzzy came to holler at him. When he came to the cell, he sat on GS's bed and looked at Freedom, without speaking. Freedom immediately went on offense but said nothing either.

Finally fuzzy spoke. "What's good with you young gangsta?"

"I'm good Fuzzy. What's up 'wit you?" Freedom said uneasily.

Fuzzy didn't notice his uneasiness and continued, "Man you know how I do it youngin. Listen though, some rumor is being thrown around about you."

"Oh. Well, what's the rumor about?" He was looking anxiously at Fuzzy.

"Word is you and the Golden girl been on some real tight shit. It ain't like yall fuckin' or nothing like that. It's just been said that y'all kickin' it some kinda hard and GS got wind of it. He talked to me about it. It wasn't a long conversation. I don't care for the gossip though, so you tell me what's happening."

Freedom sat up in his bunk. He looked at his hands guilt written all over his demeanor.

"A'ight Fuzzy. You know I won't lie to you. Yeah, I'm kickin' it with Ms. Golden. We not on a relationship status. It's more like a mutual respect. That's it."

Fuzzy let everything Freedom just said soak in before commenting. Then he spoke.

the ASUNDER Story... PART ONE: ENTER THE FIRE

"Freedom, whenever you move in on someone else's property, you should always ask them the rules. And then if you don't like their rules, you should get your own property."

"You right Fuzzy, but why are you telling me this?" Fuzzy could hear the brassiness in Freedom's tone of voice.

"Do you remember asking about renting a room in someone's house?"

"Oh yeah. I remember. That's wild, that you remember."

"Freedom, lemme give you the golden rule. Ms. Golden can't do wrong according to GS. If you two are bonding the way I'm thinking, you better be on point. I know she's attractive, but don't let her deter you from your goal. I know that I haven't made something happen for you yet, but you gotta be cool. Things like moving work in the pen don't just happen overnight. But when shit does take off, you gotta be focused and ready. One mistake and you gotta fresh charge or the wrong nigga finds out and all the wolves be at you like fresh sheep meat...you dig where I'm comin' from youngin?"

Freedom waited before responding. He didn't owe Fuzzy an explanation, but him and the old guy had established something that yielded them close. He decided to tell him what happened.

the ASUNDER Story... PART ONE: ENTER THE FIRE

"A'ight. Fuzzy me and Ms. Golden almost hit it off. Only once though. She told me that she was feelin' me and that if I could treat her better than GS, she would give me the chance again."

Fuzzy didn't so much as look confused or mad-more like concerned.

"Freedom, lemme tell you something. And you listen to me close. I've been on this camp for a long time and not once have I put myself in a life-threatening situation. You know why? Because I watch my back and never do anything to no man in his face or behind his back that will later on cost me my life. Now you and Golden messin' around? Is she worth the hassle?"

He waited for a response. Freedom seemed lost for words. Fuzzy continued.

"A'ight youngin. GS is my man. Basically, for the last few years. I practically raised this man. Now you come along, and I've felt obliged to care about you. You ain't ask for that, but I think you need some source of guidance."

"Now I can tell you to leave Ms. Golden alone. Whether you listen to me, it's on you. So, I'm not gonna tell you that. What I will say to you is this...do not say nothing else about Ms. Golden to none of these niggas."

"Now you have to step up and be a man. So, whatever Golden brings your way, you have to be able to deal 'wit it. I won't say nothing to GS for one reason only. That reason is I see something in you that will later help me. I don't know exactly what it is."

"I just know GS doesn't believe that you and she have gotten together. Other than what he orchestrated so leave it at that. That's the best thing. GS could make your life a living hell if he knew. So, don't make your bed harder than it already is. Now if she is who you want to help you endure through this bid as well as when you get out, you better be about her. Because a scorned woman is an enemy you don't ever wanna have. GS gives her security. She doesn't love him because he won't give himself fully to her. I do know this to be true. She's looking to be loved.

"Freedom, if you can't oblige that, then don't try it. If you do wanna love her, give it all you got. Everything more nothing less."

Everything that Fuzzy said to Freedom hit home. Actually, he didn't know how Fuzzy felt about the situation, but he could trust that he would keep their conversation and business between them.

the ASUNDER *Story*... PART ONE: ENTER THE FIRE

"Never in my life have I ever had someone drop jewels on me like that real. But um, Fuzzy, I wanna ask you one thing?"

"Go 'head."

"Why do you wanna help me after what I told you?"

"One...like I said before, I see something in you that'll help me later... two, you have a heart of gold. And although it's my man you're crossing lines with everybody deserves to have a chance at real love. Maybe you can give Ms. Golden a shot at that. And lastly, I don't decide on who she can and can't be with."

After they were done talking, Fuzzy and Freedom watched TV until count. During count time, Freedom sat on his bunk thinking heavily about their conversation. Fuzzy had given up a side of himself that he knew no one other than GS had seen. He had been kicking it with Fuzzy since he had first arrived on the camp. His first take on him was that he was a hardened killer, who would not play with your life if the situation called for you to leave this world. Now he was starting to see a totally different man.

This hardcore man could easily rat him out to his man right in front of his face. But he wouldn't do such a thing. He was really Feeling Fuzzy. It was something about him that

the ASUNDER Story... PART ONE: ENTER THE FIRE

made Freedom believe that everyone in the world wasn't cold hearted. He was amazed at how Fuzzy carried the situation. He just knew that he was gonna say something to GS about their conversation. Maybe GS sent the old man at him to do what he just did; however, he felt that he could trust him, but to a certain degree. And what degree that was, he didn't know.

Count cleared a little later than usual. When it did clear, it was time for chow. Freedom had caught up to Max-A-Mill. To his surprise, Max was by himself. They both got their trays which was a crappy meal. But he would at least sit through lunch and catch up on things.

"What's been up 'wit cha Max?" Freedom asked.

"Shit. You already know. 'Fo real though I'm tryna turn a rock into a mountain. 'Yo, you decided about getting' 'wit the movement yet?"

"Not yet Max, but I'll let you know." Freedom turned the conversation an entire 360 degrees.

"I wanna know if you and GS are tied in together?"

"Yeah, for now we connected on some getting' money shit, but GS want his cake and ice cream and eat it too. It's just we can't find no other connect. Oh, but when we do GS is gonna definitely miss our money."

"How much is GS charging y'all?" Freedom asked him

curiously not aware that that wasn't any of his business.

Max told him anyhow. "Man shit, that nigga chargin' us $300.00 a gram. If we buy whole weight its cheaper. But it ain't that much cheaper. Basically, GS is raping us. I mean we double, sometimes triple what we spend but it's just that. After we send money to our kids and families and shit, we ain't got nothing' for ourselves. So, it's almost like we are hustlin' for nothin.' We a big nation. It's 'bout 300 Bloods on this camp and about 75 of them is in my line up. Basically, it's about 300 mouths to feed. Everybody got families on the streets to look out for but doing that is damn near impossible. So as soon as we get another connect, we gonna cut ties 'with that greedy as nigga."

Freedom sat there for a minute or two before commenting, then as he was about to say something, Ms. Golden walked in the chow hall and came straight up to their table. She spoke first to Max-A-Mill. Then she told Freedom she needed to talk to him before he left the diner hall. He nodded in agreement. When she walked off, Max asked him what that was bout. Freedom simply said he didn't know. Max didn't ask anything else about it. They sat in silence for a few more minutes, before Max got up. Before he left, he told Freedom to think about getting down with his movement. Damn, he was adamant about this Blood proposition.

"I wonder what he really wants?" Freedom asked himself after he was gone. Freedom sat there picking with his tray. The chow hall began to clear out. Ms. Golden came over to his table. She smiled at him before speaking to him.

"Hey baby boy. How have you been feeling?" She spoke seductively.

"I'm okay Ms. Golden. What's up 'wit you?"

"You are. What's good 'wit me? Oh, but umm, do you think that you can come to our little set up we got tonight, or might you be too busy?"

"I'm never too busy when it comes to the Golden girl," Freedom said smiling.

"Okay darling then tonight. Oh, and from now on, call me Angelón okay baby?"

"Oh, you give me the honor?" He asked surprisingly.

"I don't give you the honor, you've earned the honor," she expressed seductively walking away with more pizazz in her swagger than she had ever shown.

He got up and put his tray in the cubby hole to the dish room and left. When he came out of the chow hall, he saw GS and Fuzzy. GS was talking at Fuzzy very aggressively. Freedom fell back pacing himself. He wanted to peep things out from a

the ASUNDER *Story*... PART ONE: ENTER THE FIRE

distance.

After they walked in the building, Freedom lingered trying to prepare himself for what might be getting ready to go down. Immediately, he wondered if Fuzzy sold him out.

"Fuck it...it is what it is," he said uneasily walking into the building. He went to his cell. Fuzzy and GS were in the room bagging up.

"What's good 'with cha young gangsta?" GS asked him coolly.

"Shit, I'm tryna get some of that paper too," Freedom said nonchalantly. He was just trying to check the temperature in the room, mainly GS's.

"I was just fuckin' wit you," he said putting on his JP5 player. Freedom had picked up a JP5 player on the yard for cheap.

Freedom was listening to Jay-Z Black album when someone knocked on the door. Fuzzy got up to see who it was. It was the same white man who always scored from GS. He was really starting to look bad. Shit that's what happens when you let meth break up your existence. Freedom thought. The man told GS that he only had $50 dollars, but he was tryna get a hundred piece. GS gave him a nice chunk.

the ASUNDER *Story*... PART ONE: ENTER THE FIRE

"Don't smoke everything on one hit," GS said laughingly.

"I mean that literally Action Jackson, 'cuz I ain't given' you shit else," he said with seriousness in his tone. It was subtle how GS could switch his moods up so easily. The man left the cell anxiously.

Fuzzy put the *Do Not Disturb* sign up in the door window. They had a lot of shit to bag up, but it only took them twenty maybe twenty-five minutes to do it. Freedom wondered how they moved so fast and in sync. The way they worked made him second guess himself. Would he actually be able to support Ms. Golden? He didn't think she was a materialistic woman. Or at least that's what she had claimed. Still and all when you've been living a certain kind of way for so long it's hard to break away from the lifestyle. She was GS's main attraction. He was for certain that GS had been endowing her with plenty gifts.

Tonight, he would be straight up forward with Angelón about everything; how he felt about her, what he wanted in their relationship-if they in fact had one, and what he could do for her and him if he was financially stable.

After GS and Fuzzy got everything done, Fuzzy took his half and GS took the other. They said a few more things to each other. Then they went their separate ways. Freedom was alone again. He got up and went to the door and looked out. So much was on his mind. He thought to himself that this is a world inside a world. These inmates only care about what's happening in their world. There are a few exceptions that changes some aspects, but he always had to be on guard.

Prison was like a chamber with various trap doors. Behind every door lay an obstacle. An obstacle wherein you only had two options. Either win or lose. Then if you won, what was your reward? Nothing, just another day survived in this hell hole. Freedom thought to himself that him winning was gonna be different than anyone else. When he won, it wouldn't be just another day survived in the penitentiary. He was gonna acquire the heart, mind, and body of Angelón Golden, a bond with a man who would kill you easily, if the situation called for that and finally his freedom.

After thinking about what he had to gain, he cut his JP5 player off and went outside for rec. Lil Mike had recovered from his near-death experience. Although he was in a wheelchair, he did seem content. He was being pushed around the track by a white man who stood damn near the height of Paul Bunyan and might've weighed five hundred pounds. He was nowhere near obese though. Freedom walked up to Lil Mike and his pusher.

the ASUNDER Story... PART ONE: ENTER THE FIRE

"What's happenin' wit cha Mike and Ike?" he said jokingly.

"Freedom, I'm happy and grateful to God to be alive," Lil Mike commented.

They gave each other a pound, then Lil Mike continued talking. "Freedom, this is my pusher Mr. Coy. Mr. Coy, this is Freedom."

Freedom shook his hand, which covered everything but his wrist.

"Damn!" Freedom said.

"Yeah, I get that response every time," Mr. Coy said chuckling a little.

"Hey Mr. Coy. Let me talk with the youngin for some laps. When gate break is called, I'll be over by the gate waiting for you...that is if you're not going in during the break." Lil Mike said to Mr. Coy.

"Hey, wherever you go, I go accept to the bathroom and bed with you guy. Just holler for me when y'all are done talking." Mr. Coy left them to talk.

"Freedom, the day I was stabbed I nearly passed onto the other side. Heaven or Hell, I don't know but I barely escaped death. I lost a coupla pints of blood. I had to be sewn up by an outside surgical doctor. Man that stay in the hospital for a week and a half was great. Plenty of women in tight miniskirts pacifying me like a newborn baby. The real reason I wanted to talk to you is because you probably heard the inmate version side of the story and said damn, Lil Mike I didn't know you swung that way. Anyway, I expect for this conversation never gets spoke on again. You hear me Freedom."

"Yeah, I hear you, Mike." Freedom sounded agitated. Personally whatever Lil Mike had done didn't involve him. Whatever it was, Lil Mike felt compelled to tell him about it.

Lil Mike continued. "The day I nearly lost my life was behind your celly." He let that part marinade in his head before speaking again.

"See the queen that I was in the room with used to be GS's top runner. She had GS's back like a shirt. Then outta nowhere GS cut her off. He told Fuzzy and me that he cut Tonya off because he found out she was stealing from him when she would go over to the VI (visitation) room for him and get his shit. Anyhow, I saw an opportunity and hopped on board. Me and Tonya been getting money on the hush hush for months now. GS had found out about it somehow. I don't know. GS is a very jealous and hateful man. He'd rather see Tonya broke and scrambling like eggs then come to him begging and pleading

the ASUNDER Story... PART ONE: ENTER THE FIRE

for his help. What I found out from a very reliable source was Tonya and GS had a deeper relationship besides getting money. One day though Tonya asked him for a favor, that's when GS cut her off and told her that if she mentioned any of their dealings, he would kill her. And he wouldn't leave her body. He would get rid of it so her family wouldn't be able to buy the body back from the state. You have to take his threats seriously. Anyhow, I'm good friends with Tonya's man. At the time she was in some financial trouble. So, she came to me and asked me if I could get someone to bring in the sack and Tonya would go and get it. I gave the proposition some thought, then agreed.

    Tonya was to go to the V.I. every other Saturday. It just so happens that Tonya and Amera Sevens, GS's sister had gone to cosmetology class together, before she got locked up on some check fraud charges. One Saturday, Tonya is in the visitation room and sees Amera and GS. She had already seen my folks and got the sack and was on her way out. She decides to talk to Amera. They talked for a coupla minutes before GS demands that Tonya get away from them. Tonya didn't argue with him or disrespect him in front of his sister.

    When the V.I. was over, GS went to Tonya's building and

the ASUNDER *Story*...PART ONE: ENTER THE FIRE

smacked Tonya so hard that the bitch lips started bleeding. Do you remember when GS went to the box?"

"Yeah, I remember. Go ahead though."

"Well, Tonya was the person GS had the altercation with. Anyhow, after he got out the hole he came and asked me if I had been fuckin' with one of his mules. I told him I didn't owe him an explanation and I wasn't gonna tell him shit. That was all he needed to hear. He sent the old head name Chub at me. He gave the old head $1000 dollars. Five hundred up front and another five hundred once he made his move. Freedom, GS wanted me dead. You see Freedom, GS is a dirty worker. If you're not careful, he will cross you in the long run."

What should I have to be careful about?" Freedom asked him, hoping it wasn't about Ms. Golden.

"Word is in the air that you and Golden messin' around. I don't care what y'all might be doing, but I'm gonna say this, GS is too powerful to be taken lightly on anything."

Freedom was silent.

Lil Mike continued. "Youngin you're a good dude, don't lose your life behind some foolishness."

Gate break was being announced as they were

the ASUNDER Story... PART ONE: ENTER THE FIRE

finishing their lap. Mr. Coy was waiting for Lil Mike. Freedom gave Lil Mike a pat on the shoulder and promised to get with him later.

Everything seemed clear to Freedom. He didn't wanna believe everything Lil Mike had just told him. Word of mouth didn't mean shit especially vindictive words. Maybe Lil Mike was trying to spread bad bones on GS, considering that he wanted Lil Mike dead. But how did GS know that Mike got stabbed when he wasn't on the yard?

He had to set Lil Mike up or maybe word got back to GS before they all came in from the yard that day. Impossible! GS knew something. He was sick and vicious. He wasn't scared of GS, but he did have a serious respect for him. His money was too long. Freedom needed two things right now. He needed an ally and work. Power wasn't necessarily what he wanted. He wanted wisdom.

He felt that if he was gonna win at this game, he needed to know how to handle it. Then he would know and understand how to conquer his foes. He couldn't wait for tonight with Angelón. He wasn't really eager about making love to her. Although he wanted that too. What he really wanted was to talk to her about what he needed for mere survival.

First, he needed the money, the power would follow the

paper trail, and the respect saluted the ones who demanded it.

He walked the track heavy in thought. After rec, he went in to call his family. His brother Daniel picked up.

"What's up Semaj? You call when it pleases you, huh!" Daniel sounded upset.

"My fault lil bro...it's so much shit goin' on in here it slipped by mind."

Daniel wasn't buying it.

"Semaj, what can possibly be going on in prison that serious as to why you haven't called home in almost three weeks?"

"Lil bro be easy. I apologize."

"Apology accepted," Daniel said calmly and continued speaking. "What's been going on though big head?"

"Man, I'm tryna make it. I registered for vocational class this week. The educations director spoke with me, and I should be enrolled in a couple of months."

"Damn bro. Everything we want in life has to be waited on seems like."

"Yeah Daniel...I know, but what's been going on in your world?"

"Well Semaj, I've met someone, and her name is Corin...Corin Sevens. I met her last week when I went to

the ASUNDER *Story*... PART ONE: ENTER THE FIRE

register for classes. Man, bro she is gorgeous and—"

Semaj cut him off in midsentence. "Lil bro, what's her name again?"

"Corin Sevens. Like Sevens with an *S*. Why? Do you know her or something?"

"No bro. I don't know her. It's just her last name that I know. In fact, I know it well."

"Well big bro. That's a coincidence. Maybe she has brothers, sisters, or cousins you might know."

"Listen Daniel. I'm in the cell with a guy name Godfrey Sevens."

"Well bro...I'll ask her does she have a brother by that name."

They talked for a few more minutes. Before they hung up Semaj told Daniel to make sure he didn't forget to ask his girlfriend if she had other family.

"A'ight Semaj, but make sure you don't forget that you have people on the land that wanna hear from you at least once a week, ok?"

"A'ight bro. I love you."

"Love you too Semaj."

After they said their goodbyes, Freedom went to the

the **ASUNDER** *Story* **...PART ONE: ENTER THE FIRE**

dayroom. He thought to himself about what his little brother had just talked to him about. Damn. He hoped his brother wasn't tied in with someone from GS's family. It's probably nothing, but that last name is one of a kind. Still, someone else could have the name. Oh shit! GS did say it was three of them, with two girls one he'd never saw. Suddenly, the scenery was changing up. Maybe to his advantage. He didn't want to play chess with people's lives, particularly with his own brother.

Freedom was getting familiar with the nightly activities. He had been going out at night just to familiarize himself with the festivities He was preparing himself for the day when Angelón would wanna meet him in their secret getaway again.

Spring Valley Correctional Center was a big facility. Maneuvering was easy. Unless you felt the need to be in a correctional officer's face. The only C/O he was getting to know was Ms. Golden. He also knew that when a woman sought out the man they wanted, their thinking became tunneled. He didn't know how far gone she was over him. But he knew as a man with good expertise in loving a woman, it wouldn't be long before he had her moving carelessly. He would school her though. And together they would come out as a perfect match.

Six o'clock came quick. Freedom was excited.

the ASUNDER *Story*...PART ONE: ENTER THE FIRE

After they make love tonight, he would let her know it's time to step it up Sex is a beautiful thing in a relationship, but just having sex wouldn't pay the bills. Tonight, he had to address her about making power moves.

When he had arrived safely in the laundry building, he was waiting for her to do what she had done the first time she caught him off guard. The laundry room was dark. He didn't have to move too far the first time because she was right there. He began to tiptoe through the dark hoping not to trip over anything. As he was feeling his way through the darkness, he ran into her.

"Angelón?" he said audibly.

"Shh," she whispered then grabbed his hand and walked him to a closet that had a dim light lit. She made up a small nest for them. He looked everything over including Angelón. Man, she was a sight to behold. She smiled briefly at him acknowledging her sexy body. Then she turned around slowly, so he could get a complete look at all her assets. His shaft was at attention. She noticed his manliness throbbing in his state blue jeans. She immediately went to his zipper. She undid his belt, button, and fly, then she let his jeans fall to his ankles. He stopped her. She seemed surprised.

the ASUNDER *Story*... PART ONE: ENTER THE FIRE

"Tonight, I'mma please you baby," he murmured.

"Oh...Okay." She sounded as if no one had been giving her the whole shebang. But tonight, that was all gonna change.

"Lay down sexy," he passionately commanded her.

"Yes, daddy." She did as instructed.

Then he took everything off but his socks. He also wondered if someone would come in on them. For now, though he didn't care. Love makes you do strange shit. Now that both of them saw each other's body parts, he turned off the light. He felt safer that way."

Next, he got in between her legs, licking, and caressing her as he came to her breast. She moaned out almost a little too loud. He slowly and passionately stuck his forefinger in her mouth to muffle her moans of passion, which she began sucking his finger like a pacifier. While he controlled the tempo and rhythm of their bodies, he sucked on her nipples, thirstily giving each areola a dance with his tongue. He lingered slowly down to her pleasure palace. She began breathing intensely. Her pussy was hot. He never experienced this kind of yearning for a woman. She arched herself up into his face, her wetness finding his lips. He spread apart the vulva and began licking her clitoris.

His tongue and passion sent her into ecstasy causing her

body to go into rhythmic spasms. She exploded all over his face and in his mouth. Her lady liquid was hot and sweet.

"Damn Freedom...that was delicious," she exclaimed sensuously.

He didn't stop He continued sucking and licking her love box until she almost climaxed again. He stopped. She whined out asking him why he had stopped. He got on top of her and put all eight and a half inches of his manhood inside of her begging walls. Slowly, he began easing deep inside of her.

Soon after, he began pumping feverishly in and out of her then gyrating his hips allowing him to dig deeper inside her warm pussy. Twisting and turning motion was driving Ms. Golden insane. She was matching his every move surprising him. Freedom continued his rhythm humping and pumping trying to dig his thick penis into her navel. He couldn't maintain this motion much longer. On cue, she sensed he was about to explode so she grabbed his back and pulled him down to her breast wrapping her legs around his sweaty waist. The deeper he dove in, the more she dug her nails into his wet back. She purposely was going to leave cat print scratches on him. Completely oblivious to their lovemaking, Freedom could care less if she dug the skin off his back. He finally bust all of his

the ASUNDER *Story*...PART ONE: ENTER THE FIRE

warm liquid deep inside of her. She came immediately behind him.

They immediately laid in each other's arms for a couple of minutes allowing both of them to get their bearings back.

"Freedom, I could grow to love you," she whispered into his ear. He didn't comment. A few more minutes passed before they realized they needed to get dressed and quick. She cleaned up their hideout. Then they both stepped out of the closet feeling revived.

He talked to her about what he wanted to do. She was still mentioning GS's name. He became vexed by hearing the same pathetic story line. He almost yelled at her and quickly remembered that he wasn't in his own environment.

"What am I to you Angelón? Am I just a new toy that you wanna play with until you get bored?" He in-
dignantly stated. When she didn't answer, he continued. "Shit Angelón...your sex is the bomb baby, but that ain't takin' care of you and me. If you want GS to continue to take care of you then I suggest you go back and fuck and suck him!"

She tried to smack him after that comment but lucky for him his eyes adjusted to the darkness. He caught her hand in mid swing.

the ASUNDER Story... PART ONE: ENTER THE FIRE

"Angelón, you can't love two people at the same time. It's impossible. You know why, love is the highest form of elevation between two people? You can't give one man all you got because you'll run outta love when it comes to the second man. And I won't be your fallback nigga or some contingency muthafucka. You feel what I'm sayin' Angelón?"

She looked at Freedom and finally spoke.

"Freedom, I'm scared. I'm scared of hurt again.

GS has hurt me time and time again. He's just like my father. The only difference is he hasn't beaten me or raped me like he did. Freedom, I wanna give you all of me. I just don't want you to give me half of you and the other half of you goes to money and drugs. Yes, I can bring you work. I'm tied into a connect. But once you start seeing countless money, will you forget about my feelings and my love. Semaj will you leave me behind?"

Freedom was taken back by her using his government name. He thought it was rather sexy coming from her lips.

He then cupped her face staring directly into her hazel brown eyes.

"I am not GS, or any of these other gangsta wanna be's you know around this camp. I'm one of the realists out here

the ASUNDER Story... PART ONE: ENTER THE FIRE

and with real principles. So, if you're lookin' for me to shit on you, like whoever else has then baby I'm constipated."

Ms. Golden laughed. "Baby if I'm truly what you want time will reveal all things. I'll bring you some work, but when the smoke clears, I hope we're still standing."

They talked a couple of more minutes. Then they kissed each other passionately as if they weren't ever going to see each other again. Finally, they departed.

When Freedom got back to his cell, he laid down and began thinking. He knew that eventually GS would play outta Angelón's mind and he would be her pick. He also knew that GS was a hardened killer with instincts like a pack of wolves. Moreover, he had to figure out what had to be done. GS knew too much. His money allowed him to be tied into everyone's lives he wanted to be tied into.

Once he started making money, GS would know. Would he try and kill him too? An ally would keep him in arms reach. That couldn't stop him though. Nevertheless, he needed a strong team to back him. A team such as O.M.G.B. and their head man, Max-A-Mill. In the morning he would talk to Max about his movement. He didn't want to be in a gang. He moved like a one-man army. GS was powerful, but Max was also strong. Shit was gonna wind up happening beyond his control. Plus, that kind of protection eventually demanded more money. Something had to be done though. He just might join Max-A-Mill's movement.

The saying goes...*'if you can beat 'em, join 'em.'* Then what role would he play? Would he be forced to hurt and kill people who might be stabbed with his or Max's money? He never killed a man with eagerness. The man who he killed drove him to do it.

Now that he had Angelón where he needed her to be, what would she do about GS. Would she leave him be or would she play a dummy role? It would be a matter of time before he figured things out. Shit, he already thought something was going on. All he had to do now was place his finger on it. This is the penitentiary and word spreads like wildfire once a match is lit and dropped. He thought about a lot of things that night. Reality was this...He had a lot to overcome, and shit wasn't sweet at all.

GS came inside the cell looking high as gas. He went and flumped down onto his bunk. Freedom was watching every move he made. He went to his footlocker and pulled out his porcelain plate. He took out what appeared to be heroin and

the ASUNDER Story... PART ONE: ENTER THE FIRE

put some on the plate. He got a straw out, scooped up some of the powdery substance and took a hard snort. Then he leaned back on his bunk and closed his eyes. Freedom thought to himself, 'I probably won't have to beat 'em after all. He might just beat himself.'

Freedom was gonna talk to Max-A-Mill today. He got up to get ready because today was his day. He assumed GS was at his anger management class. He thought back to last night. Things might not be as hard as he believed they would be. GS was getting high.

'I wonder when he started getting high. And to make matters worse, he didn't conceal it either. He did it right in front of me.' Freedom's thoughts were tugging at him. He knew it was only a matter of time before GS succumb to his product. 'I guess he forgot about the old adage...never get high off your own supply.' Then he allowed a sinister chuckle to escape from his mouth.

'I don't think he'll let himself fall completely off. But he will lose some of that power.'

Damn, Freedom was trippin'. This is a real-life situation. Not a video game or something. Whatever happened to GS wasn't gonna happen to him. He thought to himself. He finished getting dressed and got ready to put on his sneakers. One sneaker had two balloons and a not in it from Angelón. The note read:

Hey Freedom baby. It's your time to shine now. I'm glad that we met each other. I believe in you. I've enclosed a quarter ounce of coke in one balloon and twenty caps of heroin in the other. You don't need to break down anything because I've already done that. You can sell the caps of heroin at forty to fifty dollars and each gram of coke can go for two hundred to three hundred dollars. If you do everything accordingly, you'll see at least $3500.00 cash. Every dollar is yours. I want you to get right. All I ask of you is to remember that you have a woman now. A woman who wants you in her life, like I hope you want me in yours.

Sincerely,
A.G.

Freedom took the balloons and put them in his sweatpants pockets. He threw the letter in the toilet after shredding it up then flushed it.

'It's time young nigga...It's time to get down to business,' he said smiling.

He was gonna follow Angelón's vision, but not to a tee. Breakdown is necessary. He left his room and went upstairs to kick it with Fuzzy. He knocked on the door, but nobody

the **ASUNDER** *Story* **...PART ONE: ENTER THE FIRE**

responded. He left back down the stairs. As he was getting to the last few stairs, Fuzzy came over to the top tier and yelled for Freedom. He then went back up the stairs. Once they got into Fuzzy's room, he told him what the deal was. Fuzzy smiled.

"Young gangsta, you's the man now."

"I won't say I'm the man, Fuzzy. More like I'm that official youngin the games been waitin' to see fly like an aviator."

"Okay Freedom. Lemme see what you got?"

Freedom then reached inside this sweatpants pocket and pulled out the two balloons he was concealing. Fuzzy went to his locker and got out a plate, two blades, and some sandwich bags. Freedom was confused.

"What's that for Fuzzy?" I told you she did everything for me." Fuzzy saw the look of bewilderment on Freedom's face.

"Listen, I know what she did for you, but I'm gonna show you how to triple your work."

"Okay Fuzzy. Lemme see what you got."

Fuzzy went to work. After chopping and bagging some of the work he gave Freedom some of the stuff. He went to work emulating everything Fuzzy had done already.

the ASUNDER Story... PART ONE: ENTER THE FIRE

When they were done, Freedom had forty caps and a lot more coke. Now this was real penitentiary value.

"You shouldn't make no less than six grand...easy." Fuzzy concisely mentioned.

That sounded even better than what Angelón explained to him. He would give her two grand although she insisted that he keep the money. Whatever she might've done to get the drugs, she would never go back empty handed. She was his responsibility now and she was not gonna be a mule without credibility.

He liked what she had done for him, but once she sees what he did, she would really know that he was serious. And his mind set was...*get in, get paid, and get out*!

After everything was done, Fuzzy gave Freedom some deodorant shells then gave instructions to Freedom.

"Put everything in the roll-ons except fifteen caps and four dimes of cocaine. Take the shells to your room and stash 'em where a C/O won't second guess, then take that work to Uncle Fred and Mickey. They're in room 220. You tell 'em I sent you. You should be able to get everything off right now. Got it?"

"Got it," Freedom responded smoothly. As he exited the room, Fuzzy smiled and wished him well. He had just entered the fire.

the ASUNDER Story... PART ONE: ENTER THE FIRE

Freedom did as instructed. Not only did he make some quick green cash, Uncle Fred promised him, he'd have a money order sent his way within two days. When he was done, he went back to Fuzzy's room. Fuzzy was taking care of his hygiene. When he was done, he recommended that the two of them hit the rec yard. It was plenty of money on the yard. Freedom left to get some of his product while Fuzzy finished up.

When they got to the yard, it was packed. Fuzzy told him to give him some of the work. He was gonna help Freedom get some of the drugs off. He greatly obliged. He was kinda nervous and knew Fuzzy had things under control. Honestly speaking, he didn't mind if Fuzzy pushed everything for him.

Freedom spotted Max-A-Mill. Two other guys were with him. He approached the three of them. He told Max that he needed to talk with him personally. The men looked at Max then over to Freedom to give them a couple of seconds. He stepped off casually not waiting around for anybody this day. He was the man of the hour. Max finished up his conversation with his cronies and caught up with him.

"What's poppin' 'wit cha homie?" He asked Freedom.

"I'm good...Look though, I'm on like that," Freedom retorted coolly.

the ASUNDER *Story*...PART ONE: ENTER THE FIRE

"Like that, like that?"

"Yeah, like that, like that," expressed Freedom. They talked about prices and deals for the next few minutes. They came to an agreement. Max was a little surprised at how fast he had got on. Freedom shrugged it off.

"'Yo Freedom, if you can get it like that, then I'm willing to support your hustle. Lemme say this though. This game in the pen is serious. You should already know that err'body ain't your homie or your friend. You dig?"

"I feel what you're sayin' Max. That's why I'mma keep it in the circle." Max asked him again about joining his movement. He told him that that wasn't what he needed, for it drew too much attention. But he did let him know that he would need some manpower. Not for protection, but for extra eyes. Max expressed that he got him and no matter what happened when shit hit the fan, silence is always the key.

Max continued. "This isn't a game Free...a lotta muthafuckas die behind this shit or they turn snake but if you scratch my back then I'll scratch yours."

Chapter 4

the ASUNDER *Story*... PART ONE: ENTER THE FIRE

Take Your Time Young Man

Freedom had seen his first grand, plus a couple of hundred dollars on the second Thursday of Angelón bringing him the sack. He had two money orders for two hundred dollars sent to his books. Everything else was cash. In a way, he felt proud of himself. He owed everything to Angelón. When she came to work that day, he tried to give her five hundred dollars in cash. When she refused, he became upset somewhat. She told him that she wanted to see him come up and save his money for a rainy day, he understood. She also let him know that there would be times when things were slow, and he wouldn't make money as fast. She was proud of him though.

He wanted to know how she was getting the work without any money. She told him that her supplier was her cousin, and what he charged her for whatever she wanted was little to nothing.

Her birthday was coming up in a few months. Angelón expressed to Freedom that a birthday without him wouldn't be special. She understood both of their disposition. A birthday with him in her heart and mind and she in his would sooth some of the loneliness she had to experience when she went home. He told himself that by her birthday, he would have at least ten thousand dollars. He hoped he could see that made easy. He didn't have too many habits. He smoked weed on occasions. He only smoked Black-n-Mild cigars and he brought them by the crates. He hoped that everything would pan out.

GS was distraught a bit at Freedom's come up. He asked Freedom who his connect was. Freedom told him nobody he knew. He explained to GS in due time everything would be reveled, not by chance or coincidence, but by a devil; a jealous, envious, greedy, and hateful devil.

GS laughed at his take on his small empire. That was all freedom had to GS, a small hustle kit. GS insinuated that Golden was his mule. Freedom and Angelón knew their roles well though. And that was his and her secret.

There were so many hustles in prison, but none of them were as prominent as the drug trade. Ms. Golden and Fuzzy were schooling Freedom efficiently of all the pros and cons. They also let him know that what he was doing was not a career, but a come up. And by the end of the month, he had accumulated $5,200.00 and some change. Freedom didn't sell one or two narcotics. He supplied on demand. Ms. Golden had her hands full with him. He made him and her money. The

the ASUNDER *Story*... PART ONE: ENTER THE FIRE

thing that really made him shine was the fact that he showed her affection. They always kept their intimate bonding discreetly between them.

One night, GS asked freedom what his business was with Ms. Golden. He told GS that they had a mutual respect for each other. Nothing more. Freedom could feel the jealousy arising out of GS. But the man was a man of many faces, and he knew his role as well. At times, him and GS would work together chopping and bagging Freedom's drugs. GS would say minute shit that Freedom would overlook. Shit like...I hope she gonna keep her mouth shut if she gets pinched or ball to you fall young nigga. One thing that he worried about was when and if GS tried something. And to what extent would he take it to.

One day when Freedom came off the rec yard, he found a grotesque scene on his bunk. He would remember the rancid smell and ugliness of the feature for the rest of his life. It was a bludgeoned seagull. The head and body were separated. The bird's head was facing up looking at him. Beside the bird's dismantled body laid a bloody short note.

It read: *The sky is the limit, but you've already reached your limit. You a dead nigga*!

the ASUNDER *Story*... PART ONE: ENTER THE FIRE

He became so vexed that he almost picked up the mess and threw it at GS's TV. His mind was racing. He wondered if GS could have done such a thing. If he didn't do it, he knew who had. *'Oh, what a tangled web we weave when we practice to deceive.'* One of his mother's lifelong quotes vibrated within the walls of his head. But he hadn't done nothing that any other heterosexual wouldn't have done. He wouldn't mention this to Angelón. She might just panic. And his hustle would be finished. He tied everything up and put the note in his pocket. He might show it too Fuzzy. He took the stuff out of the cell and threw it in the trash. He came back and made up his bunk. He had spare sheets that he kept on standby just in case he had one of those dreams.

After cleaning everything up, he left out of his cell never checking any of his other property to see if everything else was in order. He went to talk to Fuzzy. He hoped like hell that Fuzzy might now what happened. As he was getting to the top tier, something in his head told him to wait around. He stopped a few doors down from Fuzzy's cell. He noticed officer Miles and Angelón come into the pod. They headed straight for his cell. A few seconds later, GS came out of a cell downstairs and went to their room. He appeared to be smiling by Freedom's take. What the hell was going on Freedom wondered.

the ASUNDER Story... PART ONE: ENTER THE FIRE

Some minutes later, Officer Miles and Angelón came out of the cell. C/O Miles had a plastic bag in his hand. Freedom couldn't really determine what was in the bag. Angelón's face told him everything. Something fucked up just happened. Freedom wanted to rush downstairs and ask her what was going on but decided against it. It seemed like all eyes were on the two officers that just left his cell. Right now, he needed to get his thoughts together.

The four thirty count was in progress when cell 206 was popped. Four big C/O's rushed in on Freedom. He didn't give any type of restraint. He knew that whatever was happening he was clean. He glanced at GS. He had a smug look on his face. He knew then that everything from the ill mess on his bunk to whatever was going on right now had been put together by GS. He was hand cuffed and escorted from his cell to the Segregation housing unit.

Once he got there, he had to strip. All his garments and shoes were searched thoroughly by one of the remaining officers that brought him back there.

"Now open your mouth?" The officer instructed.

Freedom did as he was told and opened his mouth. The C/O looked inside examining it for any hidden contraband.

"Now lift your balls up, turn around, squat and cough!"

the ASUNDER *Story*...PART ONE: ENTER THE FIRE

"Wait man---"

"Now!" The officer exclaimed cutting Freedom off from saying anything.

Freedom looked at the officer angrily for a couple of seconds then proceeded as instructed.

The C/O threw him back his boxers, t-shirt, socks, and plastic shoes. Then slammed freedom's door and left.

"Fuck you cracker!" Freedom shouted out loud. A trustee came to his cell twenty minutes later and asked him for his shoe and body size. Freedom told him everything. The inmate wrote down his sizes and left. He sat in silence at least half an hour. The trustee came back with a jumper, blanket, sheets, and special whites for administrative segregation. Freedom organized everything and laid back.

What could've possibly happened? Everything was going so smooth. He had work and he had Angelón. He even started going to church. He did a lot of dirt and wanted his life to be intact with the Almighty just in case anything happened to him.

"Damn!" he uttered aloud thinking to himself. He needed to talk to Angelón. What happened in the cell this afternoon? Why did she come out of the cell looking as if she just learned she contracted something unbearable? And what the fuck was in that plastic bag?

It was as if God heard him talking to himself. Angelón stormed into the building and headed straight for his cell. She aggressively knocked on the door of his new home.

"Get up and come here!" She exclaimed.

Freedom looked at her in a strange manner before deciding to get up.

"What's the problem Angelón!?"

"What the fuck do you mean Semaj Raymond Carter, what's the problem?? The problem is you pumping dope in your veins. Do you think for one second that I go through all the shit I go through for you to be using that shit! I can't--" Semaj cut her off in mid-sentence.

"Do you see needle tracks or any other needle lacerations on my skin?" He pulled his jumpsuit down for her to observe his flesh. She looked him up and down. Right before she was gonna say something he cut her off.

"Exactly what the fuck I thought...I still see that GS can still attach strings to you and work you like a dumb ass puppet!" Then he reached into his pocket and pulled out the bloody note and held it up to the window for her to read. After he seen her eyes widen in disbelief or he snatched the letter off the window and told her to get away from his door. She tried apologizing but he was too vexed to listen to anything she had to say.

She suddenly became ugly to him. When he looked up and caught her still standing there, he screamed on her to get the fuck away from his door. She let out a small whimper. Before she left, she promised she would straighten out everything. Then she told him she loved him. He never looked at her.

A few hours had passed, and the night was upon him. He laid in his bunk wide awake in thought. He felt betrayed by Angelón. All it took was for GS to throw some bait out there and she bit. Yeah, the great white swallowed her ass up. What GS failed to realize was the pussy he claimed was his, didn't belong to him anymore. And whatever he wanted her to do for him was done. Now he wasn't feeling her. How could she so easily be manipulated? His intuition hadn't been wrong after all. Now that he knew GS was a snake, he would keep his grass cut. He would keep it more than cut. He would burn it and when the snake came slithering across his lawn again, it would get scorched from fang to tail.

the ASUNDER *Story*...PART ONE: ENTER THE FIRE

Freedom had been on Spring Valley five months as to date. So, for every one of the four devils had embarked upon his door. The environment with the population of convicts envied what it didn't understand. The confinements and boundaries of imprisonment only pertained to the minds of the ignorant. That category didn't fit him. The envious preyed on the individuals that weren't aware of the envy around them. Some of the cowards were played or put on *Twenty-One Front Street*. Freedom just so happened to get caught up in the mix. A lesson learned by his hand. The next would be on them. Lust works two ways. It made one's physical desires more of a need and you want to cure that craving by obliging yourself with what you felt was needed. Or you begin lusting in your mind, which drives all your senses to oblivion then you forget you gave a shit and do what tricked you into doing what made you feel desirable and good.

Jealousy was by far the most poisonous of the devils. It feeds through all the four devils in a person's mind. Then releases its vices that make you sin willfully and willingly. That jealous muthafucka GS is plagued with the disease, Willing and Willful to do whatever it takes to off Freedom. He probably figured that he was green as an alien-considering this to be his first penitentiary bid. GS leaned quickly that he was not as naïve as he thought. That is exactly the reason why Freedom would surpass the opposition.

Challenge is part of the rules in game. And young or not, he is ready to take on any mortal man or gauntlet. Greed, that's some type of hunger that feeds and feeds on the prey of the predator Nothing ever suffices that hunger, until you eat the wrong shit, and you die. Karma never tasted like sweet tarts.

To become the better man, he couldn't let the uncouthly characters be a factor in who he was and what he stood for. This was a situation in which he needed to do little talking and be very analytical. He didn't consider himself to have gotten played. He was being put to the test though. And by more than one force. Nevertheless, he had to slow down and take his time. Really, he was glad this happened to him now and not later.

This time away from population and Angelón would make him better. Not so much as a better man, but a better thinker. Thought moved so rapidly in one's mind. Catching all of them was virtually impossible. Especially when you're not in tune with the things and issues in life that made you think. Because when it's all said and done, thinking was really the whole objective of being incarcerated. He finally closed his eyes dreaming of a better tomorrow if it ever came.

the ASUNDER *Story*... **PART ONE: ENTER THE FIRE**

Chapter 5

the ASUNDER *Story*... PART ONE: ENTER THE FIRE

Let Bygones Be Bygones

A whole two weeks had passed, and Freedom hadn't seen anyone, other than the normal segregation officers and the trustee. The trustee's name was Theodore also known as Theo. He was good to Freedom. He looked out on food and smokes. Freedom didn't smoke cigarettes, but since he came to seg, he had been smoking them a hundred miles and running.

Something was happening on the yard that was bigger than him. As he was laying there in his bunk deep in thought, his tray slot opened up. A C/O told him to get dressed so he can take him to the investigation's office. After getting ready, he put his hands through the slot to be cuffed. Now was the moment of clarity.

Once he got into the office, he was told to be seated in front of a hierarchy. The panel contained the Warden, the Assistant Warden, C/O Miles, a Captain, and the C/O who'd just brought him in there. The captain began first.

"I'm Captain Bailey. I oversee the building unit operations. Mr. Semaj Raymond Carter, you have been placed under investigation. On your person, we discovered capsules of heroin and a syringe. We sent the caps to the head D.O.C. Lab

the ASUNDER *Story*... PART ONE: ENTER THE FIRE

Corp to be tested. They were in fact capsules of heroin. Officer Miles discovered the caps. The syringe was later recovered. Officer Miles reported the paraphernalia, and a report was put on file. The reason you've been in segregation for two weeks so far is because we had to wait for the Lab Corp to send the results back. Warden?"

The Warden began his speech.

"Mr. Carter, in order for us to have a proper and positive procedure, we're going to need your fingerprints. If you refuse that automatically gives us a guilty verdict. Then you'll be charged with possession of a controlled substance and paraphernalia by the S.V.C.C. administrative staff. You will also be charged by the state of Delaware, which will mandatory your ten-year sentence. You are currently C Custody status; however, you may be transferred to D custody, which is maximum security. Do you have any questions before the proceedings?"

"Yes, I have one question before y'all start everything," Semaj said.

"Go ahead," Captain Bailey commented.

"Where are the capsules of heroin and the so-called paraphernalia?"

the ASUNDER *Story*...PART ONE: ENTER THE FIRE

The Assistant Warden chimed in sounding almost indignant.

"Mr. Carter, everything is in our files and science lab. Do you have any other relevant questions, sir?"

Something wasn't right and Semaj knew it.

"Yes, in fact, I do have another question. Why didn't y'all present the evidence so that I can identify what was confiscated from me?"

"Officer Miles will you so kindly go to the front office and get the things we need please? Thank you," the Warden expressed harshly.

The room fell silent as C/O Miles left. Semaj knew that whatever Officer Miles was going to retrieve didn't belong to him. First off, he had sold everything prior to the situation that happened two weeks ago, and he definitely didn't have a syringe. Second, if Angelón took care of whatever it was that they claimed they found, he was in no trouble at all.

Officer Miles came back five minutes later with a brown paper bag and sat the bag in front of the warden. The warden opened the bag and began rummaging through things He finally came out of the bag holding a plastic sandwich bag. It was only two caps in the bag and a fucked up looking syringe. Semaj smirked this was the best they could come up with. The

the ASUNDER *Story*... PART ONE: ENTER THE FIRE

warden looked at him as if waiting for a response. Then he slid the sandwich bag to Semaj so he could pick it up and examine the items.

"First and foremost, when you say on my person you found a syringe and capsules that would imply that you confiscated the items off of my physical body. Which you all did not discover the items on me. You found the items around my property. However, the drugs and paraphernalia could've easily been placed by my belongings to sabotage me. Especially when an inmate is going through a search procedure, which I must be present. Also, possession is nine tenths of the law. Which nine times outta ten chances y'all want me to pick up the bag and observe the items or maybe even go in the bag and have my fingerprints on the stuff. Otherwise, you people already have my fingerprints from when I first came on this compound. Hell, you might even want me to own up to the shit. Right?"

"You watch your tone there boy!" C/O Miles barked out. Semaj continued as if he never heard officer Miles.

"I'm willing to give out a urine sample, which I'm sure I will test clean."

The warden seemed as if he was lost for words. His

***the* ASUNDER *Story*... PART ONE: ENTER THE FIRE**

social kinetics also read that he was astonished at what the young man knew.

Semaj answered his thoughts as if reading right through him.

"Warden Wright, just because you see in front of you a black typical male, that should not give you a thorough insight on who I am. You should know that I do read, study, and comprehend very well."

After that, the warden told the C/O that brought him in the office to take him back to his cell.

When he got back in the cell, he smiled and thanked the Lord he was up on his shit. Angelón must've taken care of the package that came out of his cell that day because the sandwich bag that was in the office didn't have half of what came out of the cell. She played her role in that.

Later, that day, Freedom was released back into population. He was put in building seven which was the same building as Max-A-Mill. He was in the cell with an older Spanish man name Spider Man. Freedom introduced himself and briefed him on where he had just come from, then Spider Man briefed him on why they called him that. Freedom wasn't really in the mood for talking but fuck it he didn't have anywhere to be at this time, so he could sit and listen to his new cell mate for a while. He told Freedom that the reason people called him Spider Man was because he had gotten bit by a black widow. The poison from the bug damn near at through his left calf muscle. He showed Freedom his scar. He was amazed at the old man's survival from the deadly bite. Still his calf looked like he suffered from third degree burns. Spider Man said that the poison had to be chemically frozen and scraped out. He was allergic to the first medicine that was issued to him. The reaction almost caused for his leg to be amputated. Luckily for him the doctor was more than some quack with the profession. Nowadays doctors were a scarce commodity in prison. They talked a little while longer before one of Spider Man's compadres came to get him for the soccer tournament.

Thank God for that. It wasn't that Spider Man wasn't cool, but he wasn't in the mood at this time. He finished unpacking his belongings. After he got situated, he sat down on his bunk and listened to his JP5 player. His mind began wandering.

Okay GS tried to get me caught up. Angelón fell victim to this bait. Max and his homies were spending good money with me. Fuzzy has been like a father to me. And now I probably got a

the **ASUNDER** *Story*... **PART ONE: ENTER THE FIRE**

target on my back. Got damn it's too much going on in my circle. It's time to clean up my yard.

Max-A-Mill came to his cell after he heard of his arrival.

"What's poppin' homey?" Max asked him.

"Shit you know I'm always good," Freedom responded.

Max got going with the war report word around the street was he was getting high. The people found crack, a TV antenna, and some other shit. The story was botched up to pieces. Stories always got messed up in prison. Freedom hated that shit. He had to let his anger simmer down before he spoke again. He didn't wanna blast off on Max. It wasn't his fault. By the time Max got the story, it was probably mixed and screwed the fuck up. Freedom explained the real story to him in detail.

He didn't leave anything out except the part where he believed GS might've rigged up everything. He emphasized the most important part about the smoking crack. That was definitely not his speed, nor would it ever be.

"Now from what I've told you, you can believe me, or you can run with the idle conversation from these niggas in here. You pick you poison." Freedom finished up. He was so poised that even if Max didn't wanna believe him, he had to.

"Well, let that shit roll over a'ight? I know you good

the ASUNDER Story... PART ONE: ENTER THE FIRE

since you've been M.I.A. we had to go back to GS. I know you was only gone for two weeks, but the way the track was played to me, you were through on this spot. So, are you back in business or what?"

"I really don't know what's shakin' right now so as far as I know, do what you gotta do. Because once I find out what's going on, I'll let you know."

"Look, since you're not tryna get down 'with my set, I'm gonna say we're allies. Look, we'll make sure you're always outta harm's way. That way you won't get popped, stabbed, or your name brought up to the staff's attention. You're sora like the bank that's got security out the ass. You got me?" Max explained.

"Cool man, but what's in for you?" Freedom asked him. He knew that it was a catch to it. Max didn't act piously in his good will.

"You can cut our prices on everything by ten percent. You'll never have any problems. And we'll remain loyal to you and will run interference when needed."

"So, what you're saying to me is I'm covered on every ground?"

the ASUNDER *Story*...PART ONE: ENTER THE FIRE

"Exactly!" Max said rubbing his hands together as if he was trying to stay warm.

Freedom thought about the proposition before he spoke.

"Alright Max. I'll do that, but something you really should know just from our childhood that I never needed manpower. Right now, I'm in the fire. So as of now your reassurance on watching my back is just courtesy of what I'm able to do for you. Let me say it again. I don't need protection. You feel me?"

"Yeah Free. I'm feelin' you...but here me out. This isn't a playground like when we were kids comin' up all snotty nose and shit. This is a man's world. Sometimes everybody needs a helping hand. You dig that?"

Freedom understood thoroughly. After conversing, they dapped up one another and parted ways. After Max left, Freedom went to the cell door and looked out the door window. The story of Jonah came to mind. His mom used to read the story to him more often than not. It was his favorite story. Regardless of what Jonah went through, he had to give a message to God's people in the city of Nineveh. He felt like Jonah right now. He was in the belly of the best. It just so happened that when the beast regurgitated and you came spewing out, you better be ready because now you were in a dog-eat-dog world. The pressure was on a man in every aspect. Any day could be your last. So, when you played, you had to play for keeps.

He went back to his bunk and put his headphones on. He didn't blast the music. He wanted to be aware of every knock.

GS had to have heard that he didn't get caught up on his weak ass mouse trap. He still was the devil with many faces. His mind was vicious and menacing, willing to overtake anyone who seemed like a threat.

Freedom was not your average Joe though. He had intuition and a developed sense of precognition on his side. He didn't intend to go back at GS probably like he expected him to, but every dog had to have his day. And when his time came, he would radiate light as visual as Con Edison's energy concepts. Being incarcerated some days could be very detrimental to an individual's wellbeing. At times it can remind you of a birthday cake candle being blown out. You could be gone just like the smoke vapors that were dancing over the cake after the candles were blown out. Where does the smoke hide once the wishes have been made by the blower? And who actually

the ASUNDER Story... PART ONE: ENTER THE FIRE

remembers the wish they made days later? Just like the penitentiary life. Here today, gone tomorrow, and forgotten forever. Well, maybe mourned by some family members who hoped that you made it to the other side. The side in which the light shines and the gates are pearly white.

This dark humid and cloudy morning, Freedom will truly never forget. A terrible Tuesday he would call it if he was thinking about it on the superstitious standpoint. And why did rain make things worse? Why did rain bring misery with it? That morning had called for hot muggy showers, which did show up. His cell partner, Spider Man told him when he had first got in there that he never kept a cellie long. Shit, by the smell of things (*Things that sounded like vintage war plane propellers*) Freedom didn't think that he would stay longer either.

The guy was exceptional, but that gas; my God smelled like his body cooked fifty tortilla wraps with some old raunchy ass meat. Once he got up to use the bathroom, his celli couldn't have blatantly done it on purpose, but it was a turd in the toilet that looked like a science lab research earth warm. Sickening he thought. But he flushed it before pissing.

While brushing his teeth, he had a sharp sting on one of

his left tooth molars. Maybe a filling fell out. The sad part about that was the dental department seen you a week after you sent out your request forms, informal complaints, and at times...grievances because they forgot you had an agitating toothache.

Just when he thought shit couldn't get any worse, he hit the boulevard to go to chow. Once he got to walking, somebody was calling his name repeatedly. By the time he realized that one of Max's homies was trying to tell him to look out an old timer put his arm around his shoulder and stabbed him in the side of his rib. He didn't actually feel the stab. It was when he reacted that he felt like a hundred little fire ants thought one of his ribs were a part of the picnic raid. He fell to one knee.

The young blood member that was calling him eventually got beside him to at least try and aid him through what might be happening. At least four to six bloods caught up with the older man and beat him down. It all happened so fast. Plus, it was dark outside that early in the morning. The crowd on the catwalk never stopped moving.

The young homie helped Freedom up and was telling him to take short breaths. By the time they made it to medical, he was in and out of blackness. It was only two nurses in at the

the ASUNDER *Story*...PART ONE: ENTER THE FIRE

time. They recovered him from the youngster and was asking him for his name and the victim's name. Knowing what may come out of the whole ordeal, the younger man released his hold on Freedom and broke flight. The nurses never had a chance to snag him up. The attention had to be directed to the man in their custody, that might be dying or dead already.

Freedom had recovered sooner than expected. He suffered one bruised rib and a slightly punctured lung. Maybe a couple of centimeters from being serious yet real. GS's man was to incompetent to finish him off. The third strike could be the charm though. He only had two choices...fight back or tuck his tail and run for cover. And that for damn sure wasn't gonna happen. Yet the predicament he was in almost seemed too virulent for him to handle alone. What happens once he healed, and he had to return to the other side of things? He didn't know how long he would be in this building, but he needed to have a serious plan when he did go back. He had to strategize a means of his survival. Spring Valley Correctional Center was no joke. Exactly what Max-A-Mill had told him a few weeks ago. Max and his homies did handle the old dude like Max had promised.

They were trying to tell him to look out that morning.

the ASUNDER *Story*...PART ONE: ENTER THE FIRE

He heard somebody calling him, but he didn't pay the person and or persons no mind though. He thought someone might've been calling him to say what's up or maybe even score some shit from him. He was not aware and just that quick, he was stabbed. So, Max and his crew did have his back, so it seemed.

He needed to talk to Angelón. He avoided her every time she came to check in on him. It was actually his fault though. He'd established some type of bond with GS. Then he crossed the line by sleeping with his lady. So, when it boils down to it, he got his just reward.

"Damn reality juice tasted nasty."

He wasn't hustling for himself alone. He had a plan put together for his baby brother. And he was gonna use every element around him to make his plan for Daniel successful. Life isn't fare and shit happens. What was he to do? Appease someone else? Was he supposed to satisfy the wants of lucifer himself? Hell no!

He made a promise to his brother when he was out and about. Their family lived on minimum wages. Luckily for everybody, Daniel had gotten accepted into college, saving his mother thousands of dollars.

Daniel was attending L.I.U. in Brooklyn. His majors were

the ASUNDER *Story*... PART ONE: ENTER THE FIRE

Business Management and Arts and Fashion. His main goal was to build a prominent career from his college studies

His brother catered to women. It was Daniel's dream to start up a clothing line for women and girls once he completed school. He just didn't have the money and resources to do it. So, Semaj made him a promise if he completed college successfully, he would have whatever Daniel needed to start up and live his goals.

Although he was in prison for the next five to ten years, he wouldn't break that promise. Daniel would be graduating in four years, and then follow up with a few more years on Arts and Fashion. And when it was time to launch his career off the ground, Semaj would have that money right. Clean or dirty money, it didn't make a difference.

On the ladder of success, everybody in life used their elements to say that they successfully made it. Now considering all that, was he wrong for what he had done to GS? No not at all! And when he recovered from the dilemma, he was currently in, he would be fortified mentally and physically. For now, he just needed to get his mind right because people died every day in prison. Whether it be by someone else's hand, their own hand, or by the force of nature. What he really needed to know was could he withstand the hands of time?

the ASUNDER *Story*...PART ONE: ENTER THE FIRE

Everybody didn't make it back to the free world. For now, this was his world and home. And in his home, things accidentally happened but he was not gonna be a prisoner in his own home. It was time for him to show that he was the better man who was capable of taking care of his household.

It was a Wednesday morning when the nurse came to his cell and told him he was cleared to go back on the yard, next Monday. Damn, they believed in quick recovery. He was feeling fine physically, but mentally he was distraught. He had been catered to so much in the last two and a half weeks that he didn't put together his plan. He had so much to do and so little time to do it.

All his life, he had been a great procrastinator. And when the moment of atonement was at stake, he got the job done, barely acceptable. He went outside and did some walking. The medical unit rec yard was only for the medical patrons. So, when he got out there to walk, maybe even work out, it was a handful of inmates, roughly fifteen people. That was good. Nobody knew him exactly which allowed him to walk around alone for an hour while concentrating.

His mom used to tell him that he did too much thinking. She told him he was going to think himself into a serious brain

the ASUNDER *Story*... PART ONE: ENTER THE FIRE

freeze. Freedom chuckled while thinking of his mom's famous sayings. Maybe he should let his intuition guide him through the storm. He did do too much thinking. It was an advantage to think like he did, but it was a disadvantage too.

Everything happens for a reason. Even after planning your best, things just crumbled right in front of your eyes. He was heavy in thought when the yard whistle began blaring out loud signaling that recreation was over. As soon as he got inside, he went to take a shower. The water made him feel clean and refreshing.

The medical unit's hospitality reminded him of home. Well, maybe not that sweet, but sweet enough. It was better than being in population. After he got out of the shower, he got situated and cleaned his cell. As he was finishing up his room, she knocked on his door. He was surprised to see her. She was everywhere he seemed to be. She was determined to steal a few minutes of fame from him. That's what he meant when he said women become careless. She told him she needed to talk to him, and she would be in the dayroom.

When he got in the dayroom, it was only two inmates, Angelón, and himself in there. She was seated at the desk. He approached her. She seemed elated to be in his presence.

"What's up handsome?" she said smiling.

"Hey Angelón. What's good with you?" he asked nonchalantly. He was trying to appear not to be enthused about seeing her. He was as happy to see her as she was to see him.

"I'm ok...I miss you so much. You know I must've worried a few hairs outta my head wondering if you were alright. I'm glad to see you're doing well."

"Angelón, I'm stuck in between a rock and a hard place. I miss you too but dealing with you has almost cost me my life. I'm not saying that I don't want you in my life. Actually, we need each other. Wouldn't you say so?"

"That's what I came to talk to you about. I'm gonna start working in the kitchen next month. I'm moving up to sergeant, and it requires me to be in the kitchen. I want you to put in an application so that I can see you. The camp provides a worker's pod. For workers only. Getting in there will keep you away from all the bullshit.

"If I go to work in the kitchen, how will I be able to network?"

"Baby, I don't know if I wanna bring anymore work in."

"Listen Angelón and I need you to understand."

"I'm listening," she said methodically.

the ASUNDER *Story*...PART ONE: ENTER THE FIRE

"I have a brother at home. He starts college this year in September. I made a promise to him that once he completed school, I would have the funds he needed to start up his clothing line. No matter what happens to me, other than death. I will make something happen for my lil bro. I knew that you would get scared behind the situation. I wanna reassure you that I'm gonna make it. I know were both taking a risk when you bring in the work and I hustle the stuff. But we as people take risks every day. When we wake up. Angelón, you mean more to me than any other woman I've met, but my lil brother means the world to me so if you don't bring in the sack, I'll just go elsewhere to get it."

He was hoping that she wouldn't bite on that last comment.

"You say you care about me. But you don't really care about yourself. Because if you did, I don't think you would keep putting your life in jeopardy. What happens to us, meaning your brother and me if you get a longer sentence or worse-lose your life tryna make something happen," she said almost pleading.

Freedom fell silent before he answered.

"That's for me to worry about. I don't have to be hustling and can die in the next few minutes. See baby, what you must know is that I won't stop at nothing when it comes to keeping my word. The risk is no more than the choice because you risk dying every day you come to work here but that's your choice. You could say fuck it, fuck me, fuck everybody else, but that's your choice. And by the choice you make is the risk you take."

She signed. "I'll bring you what you need, but you have to tell me when enough is enough Semaj." she said.

After that, he looked her deep in the eyes and said,

"I don't have a set plan for how much I intend to make. However, my intuition will guide me through the tunnel and when I see the light that's when enough is enough."

Angelón sat quiet. Freedom sensed that she believed in him, but she was worried.

"You are a man...a man in who I love. I just don't wanna lose you. See I lost my dad early in life. I loss GS once I realized he never loved me. I don't wanna lose you to a decision I could've made on my own."

As she finished, the speaker sounded off for lock down and count time. She looked at him and made a kissing gesture at him. He did it back and they left each other.

the ASUNDER *Story...* PART ONE: ENTER THE FIRE

During count, he came up with a sum on which he had to reach. Fifteen grand wasn't too steep. In prison, everything you hustled was tripled.

"So, get in, get out," he mentioned to himself.

Saturday morning Freedom was awakened with the speaker box in his room. He had a visit. He was surprised. He didn't expect to be getting a visit. His family stayed completely on the other side of Delaware. If it was his family, that would be a plus, but they could've forewarned him that they would be coming. Nevertheless, he was happy, and he told himself that whoever it was they would enjoy him, and he would enjoy them the same.

He put on his new state blues and edged his hairline up. Primping took twenty minutes. He rushed to do everything. But he still felt like he took too long.

When he got to the gym, it was packed with inmates and their families. He noticed his family towards the rear of the gym. They must've spotted him first. Because they were waving him down the moment, he saw them. He was cheesing so hard that he felt like a little boy again. His mom and little brother ecstatic to see him they all hugged each other. Some tears were shed by their mom. She was very emotional when it came to her children. Semaj let down his guard and shed some tears as well. As they were sitting down, a beautiful young woman approached their table with food in her hands. As she was sitting down, Daniel introduced her.

"Semaj, this is Corin Sevens. Corin, this is my brother."

Semaj and Corin shook hands. Something about her was resonating strongly in his brain.

"Is this the girl you were talking about bro?" He already knew that she was the girl. Some reassurance was okay though.

"Yep, this is her," Daniel said as if she was the one, he had been searching for all of his young life.

After Daniel gave his brother the scoop on his lady friend, Momma Carter sent him off to get his brother something to eat.

When Daniel left, Semaj asked her did she have any brothers and sisters. She told him that her grandmother told her that she had a brother and sister, but she never met them. A bell sounded off in his head. It was too much of a coincidence. He was willing to bet his life on it that this was Godfrey's long-lost sister.

Daniel came back with the food and condiments. he thanked him.

the ASUNDER *Story*... PART ONE: ENTER THE FIRE

"Hey Semaj, your brother told me that you can spit. I love hip-hop Daniel will tell you that rap is all I like to listen to. I'm a poet myself. I can't spit, but if rap was in poetry, I'd have a Grammy potential," Corin said.

"Well yeah I spit. What you wanna hear something?" Semaj always ready to entertain the listening ear, put on.

"Sure!" Corin said anxiously.

Semaj rapped something that was family and radio friendly. It was still hot according to Corin.

"Son, you still got it. If only you could straighten your life out, you could go somewhere," Ms. Carter stated. He blushed a little. His mom always made him Charmin soft. He excused himself to go to the bathroom. As he was going to the bathroom, he spotted GS and an exotic looking woman. He thought if him and GS were still cool, he would've introduced his family and Corin to him. Intuition told him that that was GS's kid sister. Nothing happens by chance or coincidence.

As he was going back to his table, him, and GS caught eyes. GS stared for a few seconds, then turned away from him.

Freedom put up a gun motion to GS and pulled the make-believe trigger.

the ASUNDER Story... PART ONE: ENTER THE FIRE

"Yeah nigga. I see you." Freedom whispered.

When the visits were finally over Freedom looked around for GS. He must've already left. Freedom had an extended visit due to his family having a special visit. Seeing GS for the first time in weeks caused his blood to rise. He wanted to smash the nigga as soon as they locked eyes this afternoon. That would only make things better temporarily. He was gonna get him where it hurt.

After being frisked, he went back to the medical unit. His mind was cluttered with issues. Who was Corin? Where would he be moved to once he left the medical facility. The staff didn't know what happened between them. So, he could be put back in the same building with GS. Then what? What was GS thinking when he saw him? A lot had to be done and where to start, he didn't know.

Amera told GS to call her in forty-five minutes after their visit. When he got on the phone with her, she told him about the name she saw on the visitor's list.

"Her name was beside the two other names where Daniel and Deborah Carter were. I didn't notice the names at first, but as I was leaving out, I noticed the name. Godfrey, I believe she might be our sister." Amera explained. Godfrey was

the ASUNDER *Story*... PART ONE: ENTER THE FIRE

quiet.

"Well, what do you think Godfrey?" She asked him anxiously waiting for his answer.

"I don't know, shit it could be but just because she has our last name don't mean nothing."

"Well, I got her name and I'm gonna get on Facebook and do a check on her. If she is family, we'll know okay Godfrey? I love you."

"A'ight Amera. Much love to you too, sis. I'll call you next week."

When he hung up the phone, he got to thinking. If she is our long-lost sister, what brought her here to see this nigga? If she's tied into him, I need to know so Amera, do your homework sis. Fuck it though. I'll know who she is soon. And if she is who I think she is, then Freedom, we got more problems.

Monday morning Freedom was relocated to building six. A few of Max-A-Mill's homies were in the building. The youngin who came to his aid that dreadful morning he was stabbed came to his room.

"What's good homie?" He asked Freedom.
"Man, I'm good. Thanks to you blood. What's hood with

you though?"

"Man, I'm maintainin'. Peep though we gotta meeting tonight. Max is gonna be over here. I'mma let him know you here. Oh, before I go, my name is YG. Short for Young Guilly the Kid. Anyhow, I'mma politic wit' you later, a'ight?"

"A'ight," Freedom said.

He was back into the flow of things. The Bloods still acknowledge him. He was ready to get the ball rolling again. Whoever his celly was, he was white. Freedom assumed by all the pictures hanging on the wall he was white. When the young man came unintroduced in his cell, Freedom had a look on his face that read who the hell are you.

"What's up man? My name is Earl Cooper?" he said simultaneously making a hand shaking gesture towards Freedom. He shook his hand awkwardly, still trying to assess the situation. Freedom finally spoke.

"What's good fam. My name is Semaj, but I go by Freedom." A moment of silence fell between the two like a bad joke.

Earl cleared this stiffness by giving Freedom a concise summary of himself. Freedom followed up with something

the ASUNDER *Story* ... PART ONE: ENTER THE FIRE

laconic as well. Afterwards, Earl left the room giving his new celli sometime to himself.

Freedom situated his rack and laid back. He put on his headphones and began thinking.

"I'm back muthafuckas!" he said out loud listening to a Jay-Z track. Jay-Z was one of his favorite MC's. A lot of Hova's music brought out moments of wisdom to him. And he was in one of his moments.

Earl came back in the room and closed the door. Freedom was watching him. He took off his headphones and asked Earl what was up. He told Freedom it was an emergency lockdown.

"For what?!" Freedom asked him.

"Man, I wish I could tell you," Earl exclaimed.

Earl sounded like a white boy to him. That explains all the white people in the pictures. During lockdown, Earl told Freedom about his family history.

"Yeah man. I was adopted by those white people. My dad's name is Chris and my mom's name is Joanna Cooper. They tell me that they couldn't have kids and the agencies they were trying to get a child from always said they couldn't find a perfect match for them. So, when I was dropped off on their

the ASUNDER *Story*...PART ONE: ENTER THE FIRE

stairwell, they were surprised. They said they fell in love with me instantly. I grew up in a predominately white community. I was accepted by some of the white people. A lot of the whities didn't like, me. They would tell my mom things like...the Oreo cookie family, black child lover, you know anything to upset my mom. My dad didn't really care for the slander. So, the neighboring families never said things to him. Anyhow, that's the rest of my story."

Freedom didn't say anything. Earl asked him if he wanted to speak about himself. He told him later on. Right not, he just wanted to listen to his Jp5 player. Earl didn't take what Freedom said as being rude he just thought that some people are uncomfortable with just giving up their background so easily. Freedom thought to himself that Earl was alright. He was different. He was different himself, so he probably would be able to get along with him.

The lockdown was uplifted around two thirty in the afternoon. Freedom went out to rec. Max-A-Mill wasn't with his usual cronies. The picture didn't register right with him. Maybe Max didn't feel like coming outside. That wasn't logical either. He needed to see him, so he could let him know what was going on with their situation.

196

the **ASUNDER** *Story*... **PART ONE: ENTER THE FIRE**

As he was making his rounds, Fuzzy caught up to him unexpectedly.

"What's good young gangsta?" he said.

Freedom turned around quickly as if he was caught off guard.

"Oh shit! What's really good Fuzzy?"

"It's just me Freedom. You cool youngin?" Fuzzy asked.

"Yeah, I'm cool Fuzzy. It's just how you pulled up on me. I thought it—never mind."

They embraced one another, suddenly forgetting about what just happened.

"What's the good word? Long time no see," Freedom said.

"Same old shit, just a different day youngin." They both resumed back to walking. Fuzzy enlightened him on what's been going on. Freedom told Fuzzy about his visit and what he's been doing. Eventually, GS's name would partake in the conversation. Who was gonna mention him first? Fuzzy asked the question reluctantly.

"What's up with you and GS, Freedom?"

"Man, Fuzzy it's hard to say. I don't got beef with the nigga. He on some other shit though."

"You know he accused me of knowing that you were

messing with Ms. Golden."

"Ohh he did, huh? So, what's up wit y'all now?"

"Man, I've somewhat distanced myself from him. If what I'm doing is noticeable to him, it doesn't even matter. GS is very stubborn and very headstrong. What I did let him know is he needs to let you be. I told him that you are doing what he had first done when he started out hustlin' ended up ballin'. That's when he accused me of knowing about you and Ms. Golden you know what time it is with you and her. Right now, though you gotta keep her distant, but within arm's reach."

"I dig what you sayin'," Freedom said placidly.

They continued walking the track, never to mention GS's name again. A few minutes later Max-A-Mill came out of his building in handcuffs. Half the inmates that were on the yard stopped their festivities to watch the spectacle. Max-A-Mill didn't look at anybody. He walked with his head down until he was out of sight. YG pulled up on Freedom and Fuzzy and asked to talk to Freedom. Fuzzy didn't mind. He told Freedom that he would catch up with him later.

"Aye Free, the homie Max got caught up wit' some work. Word is he had thirty caps of diesel," he said giving Freedom a minute to process everything.

the ASUNDER *Story*... PART ONE: ENTER THE FIRE

"Damn!" That was all Freedom could say. He didn't expect that to happen to his homeboy.

"I'm the second in command to our set. So whatever y'all had going' on, I'll take it."

Freedom didn't know what to say.

YG started back talking as if Freedom's silence didn't mean anything.

"I don't know if you had taken a percentage off our deals. So, you just lemme know what's good and we'll work it from there."

"Yeah, I'mma see what's up with the connect and then let you know. By the way, what makes you think that I had taken a percentage from what y'all getting'?" YG came back. "Max-A-Mill told us that he was getting' shit for the low so you already know...If I'm wrong, I can stand a straightening."

"Nah, you not wrong YG, but lemme get everything straight and I'mma get wit' you." They pounded each other up and departed. Freedom wanted to know what happened to Max-A-Mill although, YG was second in command of O.M.G.B., so he claims. Why was he so eager to take the torch? And how did he know that he was taking some percentage off what Max was getting. Max had to have mentioned that he and Freedom had worked out something. He was getting it for the low.

the ASUNDER *Story*...PART ONE: ENTER THE FIRE

YG knew all the while what was going on. He had to be smart. This is a cutthroat game. The streets don't love us, but if you treat 'em right, they'll learn to respect you. Although he was in prison, the only difference between the two was you didn't have a car in the penitentiary. Other than that, you could have a woman, get drugs, have a shank as your gun, and you can touch cash money. This definitely is a replica of the streets. The whistle blew, ending the rec period. Shit was gettin' real. He did have some options. He could say fuck it. Forget Angelón although she probably wouldn't feel the same. Just do his bid and get it over with or he could ball till you fall. 'But fuck that! I gotta get home," he mentioned to himself on the way back to the building.

When Freedom got to his cell, he wanted to lay down. What did Max-A-Mill do? If he really got caught up with thirty caps of heroin? Somebody had to drop a missile on him. Dropping missile's is what came with the turf. A rat is a rat no matter where the cheese was at. The only logical thing that he could think of was somebody had to spill the beans on him besides that, Max just appeared to be too cautious and slick to get caught up like that. Max and his homies had been spending good money with him. Everybody ate from what he was getting in. Now Max is in a situation. And what was gonna be the outcome?

After count cleared, he would put his application in for the kitchen. Angelón should be in there already. She wanted him near her. The wait wouldn't be long. She told him that she would personally put his application in the kitchen supervisor's hand. When count was over, Freedom called home. His mom picked up. They talked about the visit they had and a lot of other things. But the main talk was about Daniel's new woman friend.

"Ma, I think that she is the sister of this man up here. I'm telling you. That last name, Sevens, is a rare name. You already know what my intuition leads to."

"Okay, suppose she is this guy's sister. What's the big deal?" She stated.

"It's no big deal. I'm just being nosey."

"Boy, I know when you're up to something. Don't forget I'm your mother and you lived rent free inside my belly for nine months."

Semaj laughed. "Ma, this time you're doing too much thinking instead of me. Relax."

the ASUNDER *Story*...PART ONE: ENTER THE FIRE

They talked until the operator let them know they had fifteen seconds left on the phone call.

After he got off the phone, he went to take a shower and got ready for dinner.

On his way to chow, he met up with Lil Mike and Mr. Coy aka Paul Bunyan, his pusher.

"What's good young gangsta? You heard about Max-A-Mill?" Lil Mike asked him how he was doing and ready to talk about somebody all in one sequence.

"Not really, why, what did you hear?" Freedom shot back a little irritated, however, he didn't mind listening to the latest news on his homeboy.

"Man, the trustee that works back there said Max was in the segregation office, singing like he signed a multi-record deal with DJ Khalid."

Freedom didn't say anything. What the fuck was Lil Mike, the penitentiary secret service. This muthafucka always got ears on the scoop. Freedom was heavy in thought. The last thing he heard from Lil Mike was you feel me, or something to that degree. He sped off to the chow hall.

the ASUNDER *Story...* PART ONE: ENTER THE FIRE

After getting back from chow, he went to his cell. He had to get his shit together. Everything was falling apart. One minute you're the one with the golden glove, able to box your way outta any corner. Just until you find out your gold glove was actually gold plated. And soon as you didn't look...BAM! What's strange was he knew this would be the outcome.

The last time he talked to his brother, he had about $5200.00 dollars in his account. And that was after expenses. He had done some splurging. Now he wished he had stacked up every penny because he might just have to leave the drug hustle alone.

YG knocked on the door. Freedom got up to let him in. YG came in the cell shaking his head. Freedom knew then something wrong was happening.

"You not gonna believe this Free. Man, this nigga Max-A-Spill is back there snitchin' on ayebody. They already got three other homies under investigation...shit, you might be next my nigga."

Freedom was quiet. So, it was true. That was wild how fast word traveled in the pen.

YG came back. "Look fam. I know you fucked up behind hearin' that shit. But you ain't the only nigga fucked up. Our whole movement 'bout to be checked behind this coward. Whoever ain't official tissue getting' bumped off."

"So, what you gonna do now that Max tied up?" Freedom asked him.

"For real Free, we gonna fall back for now. When shit die down, just be ready for business. Oh, the meeting we was supposed to have tonight, forget it. The only thing you need to know is that you're bullet proof. Can't nobody touch you. Anyhow, I'mma get at you."

When YG left the room, Freedom filled out the kitchen application. Then he went and put it in the mailbox. If he got into the kitchen before everything trickled down to him. He would be aware, and he might just miss the storm.

In the next few weeks, the compound did a 180-degree turn. Some key people went down. The individuals you wouldn't expect to be in the ring, got trapped off.

Freedom was in the kitchen working as a cook. He seen Angelón every day except for Sundays. He fell back for a while. Too much was happening.

GS looked like he was falling off. Yeah, it's true. He still had power, but it was becoming weaker. He would see

the ASUNDER *Story*... PART ONE: ENTER THE FIRE

Freedom and try to avoid making eye contact. Freedom noticed the signs.

Fuzzy had gotten really ill with the flu. He was hospitalized and been in the medical unit since. That was how he ducked the storm.

YG and Freedom linked back up, but the business was very discreet and incognito. O.M.G.B. was no longer a movement. All of Max's homies were brought home under another set called G Fly G Blood aka... (Gangsta Fly Gangsta Bloods).

Freedom decided that if he was gonna get in this game and bubble, he needed to take advantage of what he had. And although the tempo was different on Spring Valley Correctional Center, money still played its role. Dead presidents were the language.

When September came, he had enough money to put a down payment on Angelón's new Ford Expedition. What GS had done for her meant nothing anymore. Plus, the tables were turning on him. Freedom was becoming *Lord of the Rings*. GS and Amera found out that Corin was in fact their sister. Amera had got in contact with her. GS now knew about Freedom's little brother, Daniel. He knew his full name, where he went to college, and even had more knowledge on Freedom.

Corin and Daniel had plans to launch their clothing line once they completed school. GS figured that his baby sister cared a great deal for Freedom's brother. The way Amera said she talked about him. GS told Amera not to mention she had a brother in prison because Freedom would find out.

What GS had in mind was more than vindictiveness. He had something way more diabolical than anyone he knew could imagine. Corin was the offspring of his father's wedlock. So, using her in his scheme of things meant nothing. Eventually he'd parole or buy his freedom through his powerhouse lawyer.

"Freedom, you may have got my bitch. You even made my old school gangsta turn his back on me, but young nigga revenge is like the sweetest joy next to getting' money and bussin' nuts." GS was not at ease. He had Freedom right where he wanted him.

Max-A-Mill was placed in protective custody. He was gonna be transferred within ninety days.

"By November early December, I'll be outta this

muthafucka, finishing my time at a work camp." At first, he was fucked up about what he had done. But fuck them niggas. He came in alone and was leaving alone.

The warden offered him a plea he couldn't refuse. Once the D.A. approved it, the deal was signed and sealed. A year and a half definitely were better than what he started with. Shit he'd snitch again if he could give the D.A. more. Then he'd be home. He was still good with what he had. Twice now some blood members tried to ex him out. But protective custody was beautiful.

Max had a no meat diet. So, he was served beans. Over the years, he had lost the taste for any meat, and he actually liked being a veggie. He felt he had disciplined himself enough to do what he was doing.

Max was going to get to another spread and become somebody else. He couldn't claim he was Blood anymore. Niggas would figure him out. Snitches get dealt with. Eighteen months was all he had left. If he couldn't skate out on niggas he deserved to die. Besides, he was in P.C. how could he be touched? One of the Bloods was working in the kitchen. His name was Sky Red. They had a hit out on Max, and they were determined to carry out his penalty fee.

the ASUNDER *Story*... PART ONE: ENTER THE FIRE

Sky Red and Freedom became close friends. It wasn't a coincident when he wanted to switch jobs with Freedom. The kitchen supervisor approved the switch. Free was now working in sanitation. Easy as cake. He didn't understand why Sky Red wanted to switch from his easy job to be a cook. It didn't matter to him though. More power to him.

Freedom had slowed down on pushing drugs. Other than YG and Sky Red were the only ones he really sold to. That was all the clientele he needed.

He started catching genuine feelings for Angelón and he didn't want anything to happen to his future. Yeah, she was a potential woman for him. She had ambition, charisma, classiness, and she was a swan.

When her birthday came, he had Sky Red bake her a cake. The cake said, 'Happy Birthday Angelón on it. She cried. Later, she told freedom that nobody ever made her a birthday cake. Although she wanted him sexually for her big bash to close out her birthday. She was happy with him for being him.

Freedom was now hers and she probably would give her life for him. He loved her in a very sophisticated way.

It was a cold afternoon in October when Max had been

the ASUNDER Story... PART ONE: ENTER THE FIRE

killed. Sky Red had been grinding up glass, putting it in Max-A-Mill's beans for the past three days. On his third day, Max died after vomiting up blood repeatedly. It was a slow penetrating death. Max was complaining on day two when he woke up. However, inmates lied and bullshitted so much even a grievance meant very little. An emergency grievance was responded to in seven hours by staff. But seven hours wasn't what he needed. A couple of hours into his third day probably couldn't have saved him either. If the staff would have been paying him closer attention, he might've still been alive.

The compound went on lockdown. Once they autopsy report came back, Sky Red was apprehended and placed under investigation for a murder one.

"Damn, I coulda stopped all this from happening by turning down Sky Red's offer to switch jobs. I shoulda seen it comin' like a tidal wave. One man dead the other man facing death row. If convicted of murder, kill two birds with one stone. All behind drugs. Did Max ever give up my name? God why?" Freedom was in sorrow as he prayed. Praying still couldn't bring back the dead, which was fucked up to him. Because sometimes people didn't deserve to die. Especially in the way Max did.

the ASUNDER *Story*... PART ONE: ENTER THE FIRE

When they came off lockdown, Freedom and GS talked during the rec period. The conversation between them wasn't hunky dory either and the tension was thicker than a mud slide.

"Freedom never did I once cross you. I had and still got love for you man, but word through the wire is you fuckin' wit' Ms. Golden. So, you tell me what's good?" GS seemed too cool for a nigga that had been too adamant about ridding himself of Freedom.

Freedom was angered by his audacity.

"Listen GS, the only people I owe an explanation to is dead the other is my mom's. You tried to have me done away with...twice! You see this shit here nigga!?" He exclaimed pointing to his new but not fresh scar by his ribs.

GS looked, acting as if he was surprised.

Freedom continued,

"Nigga it's funny why I ain't popped your top off right now!"

"Freedom, you a small fry on the fish platter. Why would I try to sabotage you? Do you know what I make in a week? Muthafucka, I make what 'yo family ain't made in a year. So, who are you for me to worry about, huh!?"

the ASUNDER Story... PART ONE: ENTER THE FIRE

"Because anybody who's tryna come up you gotta beef 'wit! You've seen and heard me on my grind and your soft ass emotions overrode your intelligence."

"Alright young gangsta, you got the better hand...I just wanted to hear it from the horse's mouth." GS uttered with anger infesting his tone.

"Since I've known you, you've been a snake and a liar. That's exactly why you can't comprehend what I do because a snake can't walk. It can only slither and that causes you to miss all that's above your head," Freedom spat out.

GS smirked. "Okay young gangsta, you got it. You win...I lose. Either way, the game ends here. Basically, you do what you do and I'mma do me. Forget we met. Matter of fact, let by gones be by gones."

Freedom walked off. GS watched him with a ruthless stare. He told himself that he's gonna get a nigga where it hurts.

"Yeah, young nigga. I got you. Believe that."

Fuzzy came back to population. He lost some weight. He didn't look bad though. The man aged like an oak tree. He was glad to see Freedom. He heard what happened to Max-A-Mill.

the ASUNDER *Story*... PART ONE: ENTER THE FIRE

They had a long talk. They were both in Max's circle in a way. So, they both felt kind of disgruntled about his untimely death. Fuzzy told him something he'd never forget.

"At the end of the day, I'd rather be loved by my enemies than hated by my friends. You dig young gangsta?"

"That's deep as shit for real Fuzzy. I got you," Freedom retorted thoroughly understanding his older comrade's axiom.

"Once you step into the fire, you better always have a way of escaping...to stop, drop, and roll around won't even save you in this skillet young gangsta because shit gets lit and poppin' quick...and it ain't no replay button on life," Fuzzy added.

They continued their stroll around the yard talking about the politics that govern all of them. Rec was soon ended.

TO BE CONTINUED...

the ASUNDER *Story*... PART ONE: ENTER THE FIRE

TEASER FROM

the ASUNDER *Story...* PART ONE: ENTER THE FIRE

the ASUNDER *Story...*
PART TWO: I AM BY BROTHER'S KEEPER

the ASUNDER *Story*...PART ONE: ENTER THE FIRE

Chapter 1

the ASUNDER Story... PART ONE: ENTER THE FIRE

My Hand for Yours

Daniel had been in his second semester at L.I.U in Brooklyn New York. Presently things were coming together. His grades were considered braggard as his mom would talk highly of him anywhere, she was at. He loved his mom and with his career underway he'd build a home for her from the ground up one day.

The other lady in his life was Corin Sevens. The young ones met formally at a function the college was having for challenged youth with prodigious talent. The inevitability between them was destined and their circumstances brought them together. To him she was the "exo" in exotic and to her he was hand and some. The gene pool of inheritance endowed both with fashion minds and stylistic craftsmanship. So, the vibe between the two was signed, sealed, delivered and I'm yours. They were inseparable.

Daniel would visit his mom twice monthly and often Corin would accompany him there to Newark Delaware. The cordiality between Ms. Deb and Corin was becoming etched in stone. She was very fond of the young lady and implicated that her son and her had a bond that was solid as iron. The

the ASUNDER Story... PART ONE: ENTER THE FIRE

connection that they all had kept Daniel focused mainly on their careers, his mom, and unforgettably his brother Semaj.

He felt his brother was dealt the wrong hand in life, but he remained fortuitous through it all. Semaj was Daniel's rock. He schooled him about many perils of the shit he would have to deal with in a world of perilousness. Friends shit they did exactly what they were met to do in one's life if you let them to close and that was fry you in the end. That was his preamble in the statement of a friend. He was an inspiration to his younger sibling. And Daniel was an influence in his older brother's life. So, their connection and ties with one another had purpose. A divine purpose.

When Semaj made his return into the free world, he and him would lead their generational curse of failure into the depths of nothingness from which the lies emerged. Together they'd fulfill a lifelong destiny, only this time with a new ornament on the family tree. Corin Sevens was his soul mate and even his brother Semaj found favor in her and his relationship. Now they had something going on. See Daniel felt that a true family wasn't D.N.A but a unified body of expounding minds and people with a togetherness and each person seeking to develop a stronger foundation as the unit of people expand. They were truly expanding with the added addition of Corin Sevens.

Corin began receiving texts and phone calls from a beautiful cousin name Chanelle Sevens. Their meeting of one another was kind of peculiar at first. Chanelle claimed that she was a distant cousin of the family. And things were kind of awkward leading up to their initial contact while shopping downtown in Manhattan for fabrics.

Daniel and Corin were in the lower part of Manhattan looking for the elusive color's mauve and onyx for a show they were working on for a school project when the trio bumped into one another. At the right place at the right time. Chanelle just happened to be looking for fabrics as well.

Daniel noticed her first. Chanelle gave off the impression that she was following them when they all mysteriously appeared at the colors of mauve and onyx they had been searching for.

"Um excuse me shorty, but you wouldn't happened to be following me and my lady?" Daniel replied.

Corin finally aware of the woman's presence blushed with embarrassment from his mention of her.

the ASUNDER *Story*... PART ONE: ENTER THE FIRE

"Daniel that was so rude, don't you think so?" she expressed nudging his arm slightly.

Chanelle right on que said, "No Daniel, I'm not following you and Corin."

That comment alone put both of them immediately on guard.

"How do you know us mam?" Corin asked a bit startled. Daniel and Corin were both taken aback by her poise.

She stuck out her hand first to Corin shaking her hand then Daniel, who reluctant at first finally shook hers.

"My name is Chanelle Sevens and Corin I've been looking for you since you were like maybe four." Chanelle mentioned too calmly.

Now they both were really flabbergasted. Who was this woman and what was her meaning of meeting them really about? Chanelle gave them a fictitious fabrication of how she and the rest of the Sevens family had loss one another for different reasons and that it was only a few of them left to date. She slowly navigated them exactly to where they stood now. Damn she was good Daniel thought wondering how plausible this story could possibly be. The two cousins did have undeniable features. And Daniel Paul Corin was catching a buzz

the ASUNDER *Story*... PART ONE: ENTER THE FIRE

on the garment scene. That part she was definitely right about. She was even toting one of the DPC handbags designed by the couple. Once Daniel noticed that his apprehension eased a little, and the mood between them became cordial.

Chanelle also had a keen eye for the fashion decorum. It was impeccable in fact. Now this was a plus for the two young people because they were fashion savvy themselves but, Chanelle was sent from the heavens. She was going to help them reach levels in the industry that only the gods could muster in the eye of the needle, and this is what they both embraced.

Amera had her work cut out for her. She had to keep the story line as Chanelle always flawless. She'd finally found her fathers' deceased child and she was the golden one that she had found on the visitors list beside the man's name she had mentioned had come to see that guy Semaj Carter.

The role of a cousin wasn't going to be smooth sailing as she wanted. Her brother Godfrey had the pendulum of travesty dangling from everyone's noose. How he conjured up many of his grandiose ideas remained unheard of. Had not the situation benefitted her to some degree she'd maneuver her way from under his divisive grip. The million-dollar question was what Godfrey had concocting with some guy name Freedom in

the ASUNDER *Story*...PART ONE: ENTER THE FIRE

prison? Corin's boyfriend Daniel held a grave role in his vision as well.

So far what she understood was that the two young tailor and seamstress played a major role in Godfrey's plan for the redemption of Sevens attire. All she had to do was help him orchestrate this inglorious tune and their family will continue to flourish in the lavishness of one's wealth. Their wealth.

Shit didn't happen overnight though and if she could keep up the act as Chanelle she'd continue in the life right along with the scheme's and demands of her demented brother, somehow always attached to his odious nature. When it was all said and done, she had to be in control of everything. Right now, she didn't see the possibilities of that happening, especially with Godfrey becoming closer to the day of reconcile. For now, though, he could play the puppet master for he was the great manipulator. She was buying precious time.

She didn't know Corin Sevens, but she did take a liking to her younger sister. She was blood for Christ sakes. Godfrey told her not to catch any significant feelings and emotions too early for various stupid reasons. He felt if Corin knew the real reason behind their motive the young woman would betray them. Who the hell wouldn't? You find out your biological father was murdered by some federal undercover gangsters.

the ASUNDER *Story*... PART ONE: ENTER THE FIRE

And your oldest sister and brother manipulated you into your own inheritance from the beginning of you all's first encounter with lies and deceit. This was going to be a long ride after all, but hey she was in it to win it. Failure was a godforsaken weakness.

Her only disposition life had to offer her was fear. And she was knee deep in the iniquities of her sins. Sink or swim young scrapper this is a cesspool we all in it make your best move. Swim Michael Phelps on your best lap set the record high lap, lap, this a hard knock class ya'll in a prep school. She would become the great white.

the ASUNDER Story... PART ONE: ENTER THE FIRE

ABOUT THE AUTHOR

Born January 28, 1980, in Nuremberg Germany, Jewels Clark began writing at the early levels of childhood development. She was in a writer's course for aspiring children with prodigious talents called the 4-H club.

The youth development education program of Virginia cooperative extension 4-H is enriched with learning experiences in which young people partner with caring adults and volunteers in a fellowship unlike any other program today. With Jewel's inquiring mind, her world began to take form thus forming her ideas and placing her here in on the path of her writing experience.

By the time she was 16 years old, she could write bars and hooks that would make her native New York mother Deborah J. Clark put her in comparison of the late great 2 Pac Shakur. Although in her mind she knew with a proud mom and her conviction that she wasn't just as good as one of the greats, instead she would go along with it. She'd go on to write and compose music with local rap groups; however, that arena was just eluding to the current stage of her life.

the ASUNDER *Story*... PART ONE: ENTER THE FIRE

Jewel's experienced great stints of being a rebel only to find the uniqueness in her storytelling. Recovering from many different obstacles in her plight in life, Jewels has propelled herself into a strong, confident, and dominant woman. She currently resides in Richmond, Virginia, and hails from Norfolk Virginia.

MS. JEWELS

the ASUNDER *Story*...PART ONE: ENTER THE FIRE

Please follow Ms. Jewels Clark on social media for all the latest news on her upcoming novels.

the ASUNDER *Story*...PART ONE: ENTER THE FIRE

the ASUNDER *Story*...PART ONE: ENTER THE FIRE

the ASUNDER *Story*...PART ONE: ENTER THE FIRE

the ASUNDER *Story*...PART ONE: ENTER THE FIRE

229

the ASUNDER *Story*...PART ONE: ENTER THE FIRE

the ASUNDER *Story*...PART ONE: ENTER THE FIRE

231

the ASUNDER *Story*...PART ONE: ENTER THE FIRE

Printed in the USA
CPSIA information can be obtained
at www.ICGtesting.com
LVHW032309011124
795433LV00011B/186

9 781953 096012